More wickedly funny books by Anthony Horowitz

DIAMOND BROTHERS DETECTIVES FOR HIRE

WHERE SEAGULLS DARE

Anthony Horowitz

Interior illustrations by
Mark Beech

**WALKER
BOOKS**

First published 2022 by Walker Books Ltd
87 Vauxhall Walk, London, SE11 5HJ

2 4 6 8 10 9 7 5 3 1

Text © 2020, 2022 Nightshade Ltd
Foreword © 2022 Nightshade Ltd
Cover illustrations © 2022 Tony Ross
Interior illustrations © 2022 Mark Beech

The right of Anthony Horowitz, Tony Ross and Mark Beech
to be identified respectively as author, cover illustrator and
inside illustrator of this work has been asserted in accordance
with the Copyright, Designs and Patents Act 1988

This book has been typeset in ITC Veljovic

Printed and bound by CPI Group (UK) Ltd, Croydon CR0 4YY

British Library Cataloguing in Publication Data:
a catalogue record for this book is available from the British Library

ISBN 978-1-5295-0117-9

www.walker.co.uk

MIX
Paper from
responsible sources
FSC
www.fsc.org
FSC® C171272

Contents

Foreword

All the royalties from this book are going to charity.

Where Seagulls Dare began life as an entertainment during lockdown. With so many children stuck at home, I thought I would write something to cheer them up and the first seven chapters were posted, free, on my website from week to week. I have to say, it quite cheered me up writing them.

I finished the book last year and, as promised, I'm giving the profits to a charity that's very close to my heart.

Suffolk Home-Start supports children and families across the county. They have a small army of volunteers who visit families in their homes and help with all sorts of issues. Last year they won the Queen's Award for Voluntary Service.

I love Suffolk and I'm proud to be a patron of Suffolk Home-Start. This book is for them.

Anthony Horowitz

A Knock on the Door

I still have nightmares about Hare Island.

I get into bed and close my eyes and almost at once I'll find myself in a canoe in the North Sea with waves the size of skyscrapers crashing down on me. I'll see a vicious motorbike gang, armed with machine guns, chasing me along a road that goes nowhere and I'll hear the theme tune from *Star Wars* being played on little bells. I'll be locked in a dungeon one moment and then, seconds later, I'll find myself falling through the sky without a parachute. And when I wake up, with my head under the pillows and the duvet torn to shreds, I'll think to myself: *It was just a bad dream, it can't possibly have happened.* And then I'll remember: It did.

Like so many of my worst experiences, it all began with a knock on the door. If I ever buy a place to live, I'm going to make sure it has no doors. Life is safer that way.

Anyway, it was the first week of the summer holidays and I was stuck with my big brother, Tim, in a run-down corner of Camden Town in North London. If you've never run down there, I wouldn't bother. Camden Town has a market, a canal, a tube station and so many tattoo parlours that if you went to just half of them, you'd run out of skin. In the summer it's full of students and tourists eating fast food. The food is so bad you can't eat it fast enough. Tim's office was next to a fish and chip shop, although it was hard to tell which was which.

As you may know by now, my brother, Tim Diamond, is a private detective and he has the hat and the raincoat to prove it. What he doesn't have is any clients. The last time anyone consulted him, it had been to ask for directions to the post office and he'd still managed to send them the wrong way. The simple truth is that my brother is, without doubt, the worst private detective in the world. He's the only person I know who could get to the end of an Agatha Christie novel and still not know who did it. His last case had been three months ago and he'd just ended up going round in circles. OK, to be fair, the clues had led him to the London Eye on the South Bank of the Thames,[1] but it had still been a difficult ride and I, for one, had been glad to get off. Since then, he'd been earning extra cash as an Uber driver ... though not much cash, as he didn't have a car.

I remember that it was a Tuesday morning. That was the one that came after Monday morning, with Wednesday morning just round the corner. We were sitting at the breakfast table, staring at a miniature box of cornflakes that had come out of one of those variety packs.

"Where's the milk?" Tim asked.

"It's still in the cow," I growled. "There's nothing left in the fridge, Tim. This is it."

1. See *The Blurred Man*

"OK. We'll split them fifty–fifty." He tore open the packet and began to count out the cornflakes. "One for you, one for me, one for you..."

We might have been there until lunchtime, but that was when I heard the knock on the door. It was a woman. I could see her silhouette on the other side of the frosted-glass window, though I'm not sure it had been frosted before she arrived. Could she possibly be a client? There was no other reason for her to be here. She certainly wasn't delivering the mail.

Quickly, we cleared away the breakfast. The bowls went into the bin and the spoons into the filing cabinet. Tim snatched up the cornflakes and swallowed them, then threw himself onto the chair behind his desk. It was on wheels and I watched as it shot across the room and collided with a bookshelf, bringing a dozen Narnia books and Tim's complete *Just William* collection crashing down on his head. I wheeled him back into place and checked everything was all right. Then I opened the door.

The woman didn't walk in. She seemed to glide, as

if her feet weren't touching the ground. I knew at once that Tim had fallen in love. I could see his eyes widening and his ears turning red, which was certainly more pleasant than the other way round. It was as if he'd got his head trapped in the microwave oven. Again. My big brother wasn't completely unattractive. He kept himself in shape, even if the shape was a bit like a half-filled bin bag. But right now, his entire bone structure seemed to have collapsed in on itself and he was finding it difficult to breathe. As our new visitor walked into the room, I wondered if he'd throw up or explode. Either way, it was going to be messy.

How can I describe her? She had the sort of blonde hair you only find in a shampoo advertisement. When she shook her head, I could swear it moved in slow motion. She was in her twenties but she had the poise and the confidence of someone much older. There was one strange thing about her. I noticed that her earrings didn't match. One was black and one was white. Maybe she'd got dressed in a hurry. She was carrying a crocodile-skin handbag and from the way Tim was staring at her, he was probably wishing he was the crocodile.

"Hello!" Tim said. He gave her a crooked smile. "Can I offer you some tea? Coffee? A cornflake?"

"No thank you," she said.

"So how can I help you, Miss...?"

"Jane," she said. "Jane Nightingale."

"What a lovely name!"

"Thank you. I've had it all my life."

Tim pointed. "You may have noticed my name on the door."

"Nice to meet you, Mr Office Entrance."

"No, no! I'm Tim Diamond." He gave her another wobbly smile. "So how can I help you, Miss Nightinjail?"

She raised an eyebrow. "I need help," she said.

"Then you've come to the right place. You can rely on me one hundred per cent. If you don't believe me, ask any of my clients. Start with the ones who haven't been killed or hospitalized."

"Who's he?" Jane Nightingale had noticed me for the first time.

"I'm his kid brother," I explained. "Nick Diamond."

"What are you doing here?"

"I was about to ask you the same."

"All right." Suddenly, she was serious. "My father has gone missing."

Tim frowned. "How do you know?"

"Because I can't find him. We were meant to have lunch last week. He didn't show up. So I telephoned him. He didn't answer. I've tried emailing and texting. Nothing!"

"What exactly is the relationship between you and your father?" Tim asked.

Jane stared at him. "I'm his daughter!"

"What Tim means is ... are you close?" I said.

"He lives in Bath. I rang his neighbours..."

Tim leaned forward. "And where do they live?"

"Next door! They told me the house was empty so I drove down the motorway to check on him. One of the back windows had been smashed and it looked to me as if there'd been a struggle in the kitchen. There were broken plates on the floor and a kitchen knife stuck in the wall. I called the police and they sent someone round but I'm not sure they're taking it seriously. They just laughed at me when I said he might have been kidnapped – but nobody's seen him for days. He's never behaved this way before. I'm quite worried about him."

"What does your father do?" I asked.

"He's a writer."

"Fiction?"

"No. I'm telling the truth. He writes about computers. The history of computers, how they work ... all that sort of stuff. He's quite an expert in the field."

"Why does he work in a field? Can't he afford an office?" Tim asked.

"He has got an office. It's in his house – in the Royal Crescent – but he also comes to London three times a week to work in the British Library. They haven't seen him either." Her eyes had become moist. She dabbed at them with a handkerchief. "Nobody knows where he is."

"There's no need to upset yourself," Tim said. He was trying to cheer her up. "I'm sure there's a perfectly simple explanation. Your dad could have been run over. He could have set himself on fire. He could have fallen into a river and drowned..."

Jane Nightingale burst into tears. "I'm asking you to help me find him!" she wailed. "I don't believe he's dead."

"Don't worry," I said. "My brother didn't mean that. He was just thinking out loud."

"Well, I wish he wouldn't." She sniffed but at least she'd managed to recover a little.

Tim thought about what she'd said. "So the last time you saw him, he was in the bath..."

"No. In the city of Bath, in Somerset." She sighed. "He loves it there," she went on. "It's a beautiful place..."

"I don't think Bath needs a plug," Tim said. He swivelled round in his chair, realized he was facing the wrong way and twisted himself back again. "OK, Miss Hikingtrail. I'll search round the clock to find your father for you and if he's not round the clock, I'll look somewhere else. Fifty pounds a day and I'm on my way to Victoria."

"But the train leaves from Paddington!"

"Victoria's my travel agent. What do you say?"

"Well, all right..." She opened the handbag and pulled out a bundle of fifty-pound notes so clean she could have printed them herself. "I'll pay you a week in advance," she said. She counted out the notes: seven portraits of the Queen, which we certainly weren't going to hang on the wall. Finally, she produced two slips of paper. "This is my mobile number. And this is my father's address. His name is Alastair."

"How do you spell that?" Tim asked.

"A-L-A..." She spelled it out for him. Then she closed her handbag and stood up. "You're my only hope," she whispered.

"It's as bad as that?" I said.

"Just find him for me. Let me know he's safe."

She left the office.

As soon as she had gone, Tim snatched up the fifty-pound notes. "OK! We're going out for breakfast and then we'll pick up the train tickets," he exclaimed. "Are you coming?"

"Shouldn't you get out of your pyjamas first?" I suggested.

Tim looked down. He'd forgotten he was still wearing them. "Oh yes." He blushed. "I'll be right back!"

While he was gone, I opened my laptop and did a quick search for Alastair Nightingale. After all, if we were going to be searching for him, I thought it might be useful to know what he looked like. And there he was. He had a full page on Wikipedia with a list of his books: *The Computer Code, Exploring Cyberspace, The Art of Algorithms*. They all sounded thrilling. There was also a picture of him. He was in his fifties with glasses and the sort of ponytail that would have embarrassed a pony. He looked exactly as I'd expected: a computer geek.

And then I noticed the name.

Alistair Nightingale.

There it was, repeated three times. I looked up a couple of book reviews just to be sure. But there could be no doubt.

We'd just had a visit from a woman who claimed

to be his daughter and who said she was desperately worried about him.

But she couldn't even spell his name.

Rubber Duck

We took the train down to Bath that same day. If Alistair, or Alastair, Nightingale was in trouble, we owed it to his daughter to find him as soon as we could. Every minute that passed could mean the difference between life and death.

Our train left at twelve o'clock, which was nice of it. The departure time should have been half past eleven. A voice came over the speaker to apologize for the delay, but they didn't sound too bothered. I sat there staring out of the window as the station slid away. It's funny how cities always look the same when you're on a train. Like they don't care that you're leaving them behind.

About forty minutes into the journey, a guard came down the corridor. "Tickets!" he called out.

"No thanks," Tim replied. "We've already got some. We bought them from my travel agent."

"I need to punch them."

"Why? What did they do to you?"

I pulled out the tickets and handed them over to the guard and we spent the next hour in silence, heading west. I had a book given to me by my English teacher as part of my summer reading. It was *War Horse* by Michael Morpurgo. I'd once taken Tim to see the play and I remembered how he'd left the theatre in tears. But only because they'd run out of chocolate ice cream in the interval. Tim spent the journey with his head buried in a copy of *The Times* newspaper, which he was using to hide the latest *Beano*, which he was actually reading behind the front page.

Finally, we arrived.

Have you ever been to Bath? It looks like the set of one of those period dramas you see on TV, where everyone rides in horse-drawn carriages, the women have fans and the men wear top hats and tails. Everything is posh. You can take tea in the Pump Room. You can visit the Roman Baths. You can stroll around the Abbey. Better still, you can jump on a train and get back to London as fast as you can. The whole place is like an eighteenth-century museum of architecture but without the craziness and the excitement. There's a river in the middle and you might want to throw yourself in it when you find out about the house prices. About five million tourists visit every year and they all agree that there's only one problem with Bath: there are too many tourists.

And the first thing any of them do is head for the Royal Crescent, one of the most famous addresses in the whole country. Imagine a perfect crescent of four-storey Georgian houses. Better still, look them up on Google and save time. The houses are identical, made out of that honey-coloured Bath stone with pillars on each side of triple-height windows and chimneys straight out of *Mary Poppins*. They stand in front of a massive lawn that looks as if it's been cut with nail scissors.

The sun was shining when we arrived and it was hard to imagine it any other way. Being here was just like walking into an old painting ... which is actually something Tim once did at the Van Gogh Museum in Amsterdam, but that's another story and one I'm still trying to forget.

Alistair Nightingale lived in the middle of the crescent, assuming he was still alive. There was a removal van parked outside the house next door but otherwise there was nobody else around. I couldn't hear any sound coming from inside and there was no sign of any activity. Jane Nightingale had said that she'd found a window broken at the back so that's where we began. Only then did I realize that we hadn't been given a key to the house, which was quite strange when you think about it. Surely she'd have expected us to take a look around? To make things worse, the back window had been boarded up. The other windows were barred. Suddenly, it looked as if the whole journey down here was going to be a waste of time. How were we supposed to get in?

Tim had had the same thought. "We're going to need a paper clip," he said.

"Why?"

"I can pick the lock in the front door."

That made me smile. Tim couldn't pick a quarrel, let alone a lock. For his birthday once I'd taken him to one of those "escape rooms" and he'd still been there a week later ... trying to find his way *in*.

Even so, we went round to the front again just in case the cleaner or somebody had accidentally left the main door open. We were out of luck. The door was locked, a thick slab of English oak bolted into a solid stone frame. The windows on either side were sealed tight. A paper clip wasn't going to get us into the house. A stick of dynamite would be more helpful.

"Let's ring the doorbell," I suggested.

"Are you crazy?" Tim stared at me. "Somebody might hear it!"

"That's the whole idea, Tim. If someone's inside, they might open the door and let us in."

Tim knelt down. There was a metal flap on a spring

over the letter box. He pushed it up and looked through.

"What can you see?" I asked.

"Nudding."

"Is there anyone there?"

"I don't dink so."

"Tim ... have you got your nose trapped in the letter box?"

Tim let out a little sob and I leaned over him, pushed the flap open again and released him. He stood up, rubbing his nose. "De house is ebty," he said.

I was almost tempted to give up when the door of the neighbouring house opened and two men came out, carrying a piano. Staggering under the weight, they headed for the removal van that I'd noticed parked outside. Maybe the owners were moving or maybe they were being burgled, but either way I saw an opportunity. I grabbed hold of Tim. "Quickly!" I whispered.

Before he could argue, I'd dragged him along the pavement and into the neighbouring house. The two removal men, or burglars, were bowed by the weight of the piano they were lifting into their van and didn't see us. We passed through the door and into the hall, our feet making no sound on the luxury carpet that was about six inches thick. There was a flight of stairs ahead of us and I made for it without pausing, glimpsing expensive furniture, a chandelier, the sort of modern art that could be hung upside down without anyone noticing. Whoever lived here was rich. If their piano had just been stolen, they probably wouldn't even notice and when they did they'd just nip out and buy another.

We made it to the first floor, which was as expensive as the ground floor, only higher up. I glanced through an open door and saw a housekeeper making a bed. Fortunately, she had her back to us. I was looking for a second staircase and found it at the far end. It led me all the way up to the roof, which was exactly what I wanted. We came to a door at the very top and burst out into the open air.

"What are we doing up here?" Tim panted. "You've got it all wrong, Nick. This isn't where Wensleydale lives!"

"It's Alistair Nightingale, Tim. And I know he lives

next door. But maybe we can find a way in from up here."

We were standing behind a stone balustrade – it was all that separated us from the ground, which was a long way below. I hoped Tim wouldn't look down. Heights were just one of the things he was scared of – along with spiders, jellyfish, guns, flying, injections, his own shadow, dentists, the dark ... and death. A grey-tiled roof slanted up behind and here's the thing: every house in the Royal Crescent has a separate roof, but there's just a low barrier between them, so we could easily step from one to another. I was hoping for a door like the one we had come through but I could already see that there wasn't one. Nightingale's roof looked in bad repair with some of the tiles missing. Someone had placed a sign in the middle that read "DANGER".

"I don't see any danger," Tim said, taking a step towards it.

"Wait...!" I began.

Too late. With a brief cry, Tim had disappeared.

The roof was worse than I'd thought. Rot or damp must have weakened the structure and, unable to support his weight, a large section of it had collapsed under his feet. I hurried forward and looked through the hole he had just made. Tim was lying on his back in what looked like an attic room, surrounded by dust and debris and with an angry-looking pigeon watching him from the side. I wasn't sure where it had come from but I hoped Tim hadn't seen it. He was scared of pigeons too.

Tim stood up. "I found a way in!" he said.

"That's brilliant, Tim!" I lowered myself down and joined him. "Anything broken?"

"Only the roof!"

"Yeah. Well, let's get moving."

The strange thing was that Alistair Nightingale's home was the complete opposite of his neighbours'. It was dark and shabby with threadbare carpets and furniture that could have come out of a junkyard, and if it were mine, I'd have definitely sent it back again. There was mess everywhere: old clothes in the bedrooms, damp towels and worn-out toothbrushes in the bathroom, unwashed plates in the kitchen. The whole place smelled as if the owner had never gone out.

In a corridor there was a tray of cat litter that needed emptying, but no sign of a cat. The same damp that had attacked the roof was coming through the walls.

The only modern touch I noticed as we came out of the attic was a CCTV camera mounted in the ceiling, blinking as it watched us with its single glass eye. In fact, there were cameras throughout the house and that made me uneasy. It was always possible that someone could be watching us right now from a distant location. Maybe Nightingale himself was on the other side of a TV monitor. You know the nasty feeling you get when you think you're being watched? It's a whole lot nastier when you know it for certain.

Even so, we searched the place from top to bottom, starting on the top floor, which had three guest rooms but no guests. Nightingale must have slept in the master bedroom on the second floor. The sheets on the bed were crumpled and a soft toy poked out from under the pillows. There was a library opposite, full of books about computers and programming, some of them written by Nightingale himself. A picture of the Beatles – one of their record covers – hung on the wall and that seemed out of keeping with the rest of the place, but this was clearly where Nightingale did his writing. He had a desk piled high with printouts that made no sense to me. Two ashtrays sat side by side, overflowing with about a hundred cigarette butts. Why does anybody smoke? The foul smell of old tobacco wrapped its arms around us as we worked our way through the mess. Tim's eyes were bulging and, for a moment, I thought he'd seen something shocking. Then I realized he was trying not to breathe.

The kitchen was another disaster area, with one window boarded up, broken plates on the floor and a knife jutting out from the wall, just as Jane Nightingale had described. A door led into the largest room in the house. There was a long trestle table in the middle and it was jammed with electronic equipment, which, like the CCTV cameras, looked brand new. I'd never seen so many computers – mainframes as well as laptops – screens and keyboards, hard drives, scanners and printers all tangled together on the wooden surface. I don't know how much this stuff must have cost, but apart from an Amazon Alexa connected to two speakers, all of it seemed pretty sophisticated – not the sort of stuff you'd find in your local high street.

Half a dozen more ashtrays spilling out cigarette ends sat among all this and there were old clothes as well as cartons and boxes from fast-food deliveries, many of them with food still inside. Nightingale liked pizza, curry and doughnuts. I wondered what he would look like, if I ever got to meet him. All I'd seen of him from the photos was his face.

There was one other thing that was weird about the house, although it had taken me a while to notice. The floor of the computer room was made of plain wooden boards but there was a zebra-skin rug in the middle and, seeing it, I remembered the Beatles picture hanging in the library. It had shown the Fab Four walking across Abbey Road. On a zebra crossing. And the stuffed animal in the bedroom had been a toy zebra.

So what was that all about?

Something else puzzled me. Jane Nightingale had said it looked like there had been a struggle, which is why she thought her father had been kidnapped. But the truth is, you could have had a full-scale war in this house and it would have been hard to tell it had happened. That knife in the wall, for example. Did it suggest a fight or had Nightingale just stuck it there because he couldn't be bothered to put it back in the drawer?

One thing was certain. We weren't going to find anything here. There might be a clue in the house. There might be a thousand of them. But how could we possibly find them in all this chaos?

Tim reached out for a piece of cloth that was resting on the arm of a sofa and blew his nose. "He's not here," he said. "There's absolutely no sign of him."

"Except for his underpants," I agreed.

"Where are they?"

"You've just used them to blow your nose."

Tim gagged and dropped them on the floor. "What are we going to do?" he asked.

"Well, I suppose we could speak to the neighbours..."

That was as far as I got. We both heard it at the same time: a key turning in a lock. Somebody was opening the front door. Then there was a low murmuring as two men let themselves in. It was impossible to hear what they were saying but somehow I already knew they meant trouble. I've met a lot of crooks in my time and they all talk the same way, spitting out the words like bullets. Many of them can't even say "Good morning. How are you?" without it coming across like a death threat.

These two sounded particularly unpleasant. And they were heading further into the house.

"OK." Tim put his finger to his lips and hissed: "Whatever you do, Nick, don't make a sound."

"Right," I said.

He took a step back, looking for somewhere to hide and, at that moment, his elbow knocked into an empty wine bottle, which tottered and then fell towards the wooden floor. Tim screeched. He reached out with both hands to grab it, missed and as the bottle shattered, his elbow caught the corner of the trestle table, which immediately collapsed, crashing down with about a ton of computers and all the other equipment in an explosion of grinding metal and shattering glass. Two of the computer screens had been smashed to pieces. The other computer, which was still plugged in, short-circuited and exploded. Somehow, the Alexa self-activated and the opening bars of Beethoven's Fifth Symphony blasted out of the speakers before there was another shower of sparks and silence returned.

The two of us stood there, paralysed.

"Do you think they heard us?" Tim whispered.

"Move!" We had nowhere to go. There was only one door, leading back into the kitchen, and if we went that way, we'd definitely be seen. However, I'd noticed an archway covered by a curtain on one side of the room. I threw the curtain back to find an empty space behind it. I grabbed hold of Tim and pushed him in. Then I followed, pulling the curtain back just as the two men came hurrying in.

I'd left a crack between the curtain and the wall, which was just wide enough for me to look through and, although they couldn't see me, I had a clear view of the new arrivals. I felt my heart sink. They were bad news all right. It wasn't the broken noses, the sunglasses, the shaven heads or the beards. It wasn't the rippling muscles or the tattoos ... the cobras crawling up their arms, the daggers on the sides of their necks. It wasn't even the matching black leather biker jackets with the letters "WC" printed in silver studs. No. What I was staring at was the massive guns that they were both carrying as they looked around them for somebody to shoot.

They certainly weren't tourists. That much was clear.

"You hear that, Tommy?" one of them asked. He had a high-pitched voice that seemed to come out of his nose as if he had forgotten he actually had a mouth.

"I definitely heard something, Troy," the other man replied. He spoke slowly as if he had to work out what word was coming next. "And I think it came from this room."

"Someone's hiding."

"That's what I thought. That's my view entirely."

"Well, since nobody came out, they must still be in here. I think we should find them and kill them."

"Why don't we kill them first and find them later?"

"No, Tommy. I think my way's best."

"All right, Troy. Whatever you say. But where are they hiding?"

The two men scanned the room. One of them – Troy – was scratching his beard. But the other one – Tommy – had noticed the curtain. He was looking straight at me, even if he hadn't seen me yet. "There's a curtain!" he exclaimed.

"That's true," Troy agreed.

"Maybe they're hiding behind it!"

"Good work, Tommy. Let's fire lots of bullets through the material and then we can have a look."

"That's exactly what I was going to suggest, Troy."

"Right!"

They both lifted their guns and took aim. There was absolutely nothing we could do. It didn't seem fair. We'd only been hired that morning and now we were about to be shot to pieces. We hadn't even made it to teatime.

But then there was a loud *miaow* from the other side of the room and both the killers twisted round as a fluffy ginger cat padded forward, making its way through the broken equipment. I'd noticed the cat litter upstairs.

Now, finally, the cat had made an appearance.

Troy lowered his gun and laughed. "That's what made all the noise!" he exclaimed. "It was the cat!"

Tommy was less cheerful. "Shall we kill it?" he asked.

"Why would we want to do that?" Troy asked.

"It might be a foreign cat. It might be Siamese or Burmese or something like that."

"It looks like an ordinary English cat to me," Troy said. "Let's not waste any more time, Tommy. Also, bullets aren't cheap. I say we find this rubber duck thing and get out of here."

Rubber duck thing. What were they talking about?

"Where did he say it was?" Tommy asked.

"It fell out of his pocket. He thought it was over by the door."

"Here it is!" Tommy had leaned down, showing an enormous bottom, the sort that would have embarrassed a builder. When he straightened up, he was holding something in his hand but I couldn't see what it was. "Mission accomplished!" he went on.

"Then let's get out of here."

"The boss told us to call him if we found it."

"You're right, Troy. He did." Tommy reached into his back pocket. He was wearing horrible jeans. They were shapeless, colourless and filthy. They really suited him. He took out a mobile phone and glanced at it. "I haven't got a signal," he whined.

"All right. All right." Troy took out his phone and tried to dial. He examined the screen. "My battery's dead," he complained.

"So what are we going to do now?"

Troy looked around him. His eyes lit up. "There's a landline!" he exclaimed. I hadn't noticed it before but there was an ordinary telephone on a table by the door. Troy snatched it and dialled. I watched carefully. Tim was leaning over my shoulder, doing the same.

It took about ten seconds. Then Troy was connected.

"We found the rubber duck!" he shouted.

The voice at the other end spoke for a few seconds.

"All right! We'll send it to you on the island."

He hung up and without saying another word, the two men walked out.

I waited until I heard the front door open and close, then Tim and I emerged from behind the curtain. "That was close!" I said.

"Yes," Tim agreed. "They almost shot the cat!"

I hadn't been thinking about the cat. "What do you reckon that was all about?" I asked.

"They came to Bath for a rubber duck..."

"It had fallen out of his pocket. That was what they said."

"And they came all the way from Ireland!"

"No, Tim. They said they were going to send it to an island ... but that could be anywhere." I tried to collect my thoughts. "I wonder who they rang..."

"Maybe we can ring the operator."

"Maybe we don't need to."

I snatched up the telephone. It felt odd to be holding an old-fashioned receiver in my hand but maybe Alistair Nightingale thought a landline was safer. I'd remembered something. I found the REDIAL button and hit it.

The telephone automatically called the number but this time nobody answered. It went straight to voice-mail. I listened for about half a minute. Then I hung up.

Tim was staring at me. "Who was it?" he demanded. "Who did they call?"

"I don't get it," I said. "They rang St Paul's Cathedral in London."

"Maybe it was a wrong number."

"No." I shook my head. "It was definitely the number they dialled." I put the phone down. "They spoke to the Archbishop."

Fortune Cookies

"Hello, you have reached St Paul's Cathedral and the office of the Archbishop of London. Please leave a message after the chimes – or press the hashtag if you've taken a vow of silence – and we'll get back to you. Thank you."

That was the message I'd heard when I'd made the call from Alistair Nightingale's home. It was a man's voice that clicked off at the end, followed by a short burst of church bells and a gospel choir in the background.

"It doesn't make any sense," I said.

Tim and I were back at the office. It was early

evening and we'd ordered dinner from our local Chinese takeaway, which had arrived complete with chopsticks and fortune cookies.

"What do you mean?" Tim asked.

"I'm talking about the case, Tim. There are things I don't understand."

"Like what?"

"Well, let's start with the rubber duck."

"No thanks. I've already had some."

"The rubber duck that Troy and Tommy picked up in the computer room. What was that all about? And why did they want to kill us?"

"Lots of people want to kill me."

"But normally, they wait until they get to know you. These guys were ready to shoot both of us down without even seeing our faces. And there was the cat..."

"No, Nick. The cat didn't want to kill us."

"They were about to shoot it. You heard what they said. But because it was English, they left it alone. And finally, why did they telephone the Archbishop of London?"

"Well, it was faster than writing him a letter..."

"Why contact him at all?"

We weren't going to get anywhere talking about it so we finished the meal in silence. At the end we cracked open the fortune cookies. You must know what I'm talking about: those little crescent-shaped biscuits with a slip of paper hidden inside, telling your fortune. The messages are usually vague. They make you smile.

Not these ones.

Mine said: *If you poke your nose in other people's business, you will lose your nose.* And Tim's was even worse: *Drop the case or you will be violently murdered.*

Tim stared at the strip of paper lying in his hand. "That's not very nice," he muttered.

For once I had to agree. If I hadn't already eaten, it would have quite put me off my food. I went to bed about half an hour later but it was a while before I got any sleep.

I was still thinking about the two messages the next morning when I got up and went to clean my teeth. Had they been sent to us deliberately or did the Chinese takeaway have a general policy of terrifying its customers? Looking at myself in the bathroom mirror, I was tempted to give up on the case altogether. I was too young for all this. My friends were spending the summer holidays at the seaside, camping, at Disneyland and all the rest of it. Why should I be the one chasing around England, avoiding bearded maniacs with guns while trying to track down someone I'd never even met?

But I couldn't leave Tim on his own. That was the truth of it. He might be twice my age, but left to himself he'd have almost zero chance of making it to the end of the day. He'd actually be doing pretty well if he got as far as lunchtime.

And I couldn't drop the case. Jane Nightingale had hired us to find her missing father and from what we had learned so far, it looked as if he might be in danger. Worse still, she might ask for the money back.

The sum of £350 may sound like a lot but we'd already spent a chunk of it on two meals and train tickets, and Tim owed six weeks' rent. I also needed a new school uniform. The one I was wearing looked ridiculous on me – it belonged to a different school.

So, after breakfast, we called the Archbishop's office again and this time we were lucky. A man answered. He had one of those posh voices that belong to someone who's much cleverer than you and who wants you to know it.

"Hello?" he said. "May I ask who is speaking?"

"Yes, you may!" Tim replied.

"So, who is speaking?"

"Well ... you are!" Tim said.

I groaned and snatched the phone. "Hi," I said. "My name is Nick Diamond. Are you the Archbishop of London?"

"No, no. I'm Derek Winslow, the Archbishop's Chief of Staff. How can I help you?"

This was tricky. If I told him everything that had happened in Bath, he might think I was crazy and ring off. So I explained that we were looking for a man called Alistair Nightingale who had disappeared and that we believed he was in some way connected with the Archbishop's office.

"I can't say I know anyone called Alistair Nightingale," Winslow replied. "May I ask how you got this number?"

"Two friends of his called you yesterday. Tommy and Troy. They seemed to think you might know where he was."

"This is all very strange." Winslow sounded flustered.

Tim had been leaning over me, listening to all this, and before I could stop him, he snatched the phone away. "All right, Hounslow," he said. Then he realized he was talking into the earpiece and turned the phone round. "All right, Hounslow," he repeated. "If you can't help us, maybe we should talk to someone who can. How about the Archbishop?"

"You can't meet the Archbishop. He's at a christening."

"Doesn't he have a name?"

"He's doing the christening! I'm afraid he's too busy to meet you."

I grabbed the phone back. "We believe Mr Nightingale is in danger," I said. "We really need to talk to you."

There was a minute's silence at the end of the line. I thought we'd been cut off but then Winslow spoke again. "I'll meet you if you insist, although I don't see how I can help you..."

He gave me an address and we set out at once, taking the tube down to St Paul's station in central London. The Archbishop's office was set in an elegant red-brick building called the Chapter House, which was on the other side of a walkway right next to the Cathedral itself. The door opened into a hallway with a nun sitting behind a reception desk. She was quite elderly, dressed in black with a white cowl over her head and a cross around her neck. I could hear religious music playing quietly in the background.

"Good morning." She greeted us with a smile.

"We have a meeting with Derek Winslow," I explained.

The nun pointed. "He's gone upstairs," she said.

"You mean – he's dead?" Tim asked.

"No. He's in his office. On the third floor. He's expecting you."

Tim leaned forward and eyed her suspiciously. "How did he know we were coming?" he demanded.

The nun looked puzzled. "You asked for an appointment, my son! You rang him this morning!"

"That's right." I grabbed hold of Tim. "Thank you."

We walked over to the stairs. "You can't get into a fight with a nun!" I whispered.

Tim frowned. "What makes you think she is a nun?"

We climbed up to a neat square office with views of the Cathedral. It was simply furnished with a desk, two chairs for visitors and a table with a lamp. The pictures on the walls showed scenes from the Bible. The man behind the desk was small, bald and pink-cheeked with half-moon glasses hanging on a cord. I guessed he was about forty years old. He was dressed in a suit that didn't look much younger.

I took a seat. Tim sat down next to me.

"I'm afraid I can't give you very much of my time," Winslow began.

"We don't need any of your time, Windsock," Tim growled. "We just need answers. Did you get a phone call yesterday?"

"My name is Winslow." The man's cheeks had gone a little pinker. "And I received a great many phone calls yesterday. I look after the Archbishop's diary and I can assure you it's a very busy one. People are asking for him all the time."

"My brother's a private detective," I explained. "Yesterday we were in Bath and we were held up by two gangsters. We know that they rang this office."

"That seems very unlikely," Winslow replied. "I deal exclusively with the Archbishop's religious and business affairs..."

"Does he know any gangsters?" Tim asked.

"He knows many sinners, but he would not speak to anyone who had broken the law." Winslow turned back to me. "Are you sure you have the right number?"

I'd brought it with me, written down on a sheet of paper, and I slid it onto the desk for him to see.

He frowned. "Well, this is very strange," he continued. "I can't deny that this is my number. But I can assure you, I didn't take a call from ... what did you say their names were?"

"Tommy and Troy," I said.

Winslow shook his head. He had pale blue eyes that seemed to be hiding behind his glasses, as if they were afraid. "I don't..." he began. Then something occurred to him. "Wait a minute ... Tommy and Troy!"

"You know them?" I asked.

"No. But we had two builders here last week. They came in to fix the old boiler."

Tim frowned. "You mean ... the lady downstairs?"

"No, Mr Diamond. The boiler for the central heating. Not that we need it during the summer, of course, but even so we have to have hot water and the boiler broke quite unexpectedly. They very kindly came in from the building site across the road."

"Can you describe them?" I asked.

"I'm afraid I didn't see them. One of the sisters let them in..."

"How many sisters do you have, Mr Windchime?"

"I'm talking about the nuns. They dealt with it. And now that I think about it, I believe their names were Thomas and Troy. Or something like that."

"Across the road...?" I looked out of the window but all I could see was the Cathedral.

"It's just a few minutes from here. In Cannon Street."

I didn't get it. First of all, I'd mentioned the two names when I'd called Winslow just over an hour ago and they hadn't meant anything to him then. So what had happened now to make all the difference? And secondly, it didn't add up. If you needed to get some-one in to fix a boiler, wouldn't you just call a plumber? It seemed more than a bit odd to go knocking on the door of a local building site ... assuming they'd got round to building the doors, that is.

But right then, there was no other explanation. Derek Winslow looked completely harmless. And not just that – he was a senior official in the Church of England, sitting in a smart office next to one of the world's most famous cathedrals. We had no choice but to believe him, and anyway, how could it possibly hurt us to stroll down to a nearby building site?

We found the building site easily enough. If you've ever been to London, you'll know that they're putting up new office buildings daily. There are cranes on every street corner helping to build new corners on every street. The Shard, the Gherkin, the Walkie Talkie ... you only have to blink and you'll walk slap bang into a wall that wasn't there the day before.

It took us less than five minutes, walking down towards the Thames, before we came across the huge metal and concrete skeleton that was soon going to be "London's most exciting new workspace". At least, that's what the sign said. About fifty men and women in yellow jackets and hard hats were swarming over the site. A huge crane was lifting a metal girder, inch by inch, into the sky. A cement lorry had been parked in the middle of the rubble and was spewing out grey sludge. There were safety officers, delivery drivers, security staff ... all hard at work on the other side of the fence. Even if Tommy and Troy were somewhere here, it would be impossible to find them.

Tim had come to the same conclusion. "Hopeless," he muttered.

"Don't be so hard on yourself," I said.

He shook his head. "There's no way they're going to let us in. Let's go home, kid. We can—"

He never got to the end of the sentence.

It was the shadow that saved our lives. This was a bright summer's day and I'd been looking at the builders through a glare of sunlight. But suddenly I was aware of something dark cutting across my vision and I knew it could only mean one of two things. Either there had been an unexpected eclipse of the sun, or a large object was hurtling down towards us at a terrifying speed. I decided on the second option.

I threw myself at Tim. The two of us had been standing on the edge of the pavement, looking across the road, but now my shoulder crashed into his stomach and the two of us went sprawling. I think I heard him protest but I had carried him with me, away from the road and up against the side of the nearest building, which happened to be a supermarket. I looked up just in time to see the end of the world. And it was heading straight for me.

It was the steel girder. A moment before, it had been attached to the crane. Now it was plunging out of the sky, plummeting towards us.

There was an explosion like nothing I'd ever experienced. It wasn't just the noise, although that was deafening. The entire city and even the sky vanished, disintegrating into a cloud of dust and debris. All the air seemed to have been sucked into a black hole. The supermarket's alarm had gone off and there was a howling sound nearby, either a dog or another alarm. Cars were hooting. People were screaming. At some stage I must have closed my eyes. With difficulty, I opened them and saw the pavement. It was pressing itself against my cheek.

"Tim...?" I whispered. It was impossible to shout with all the dust in my throat.

He coughed. "Why did you knock me over?" he demanded.

There was no answer to that. I wiped a hand across my eyes, trying to clear my vision. I could feel tears trickling down my cheeks. Maybe it was relief. I looked up and saw a great slab of metal, a steel girder three metres long, slanting up from the pavement. I squeezed myself round it and somehow managed to get to my feet. As I stood up, it was like climbing out of a volcanic crater, back into the modern world.

One way or another, I worked out what had happened.

When we had first arrived, I had seen the girder, which must have weighed at least a ton. For some reason, the crane operator had decided to drop it on top of us. Or maybe he'd just been a little clumsy. That was the shadow I'd seen. The girder hadn't actually been released. It had just been lowered very fast, still attached to the crane. At the last moment, the girder had wedged itself against the front wall of the supermarket. It was a miracle that nobody had been hurt. A parked car had been crushed, part of the pavement had shattered and it was going to be a while before anyone got a two-for-one special offer at the supermarket, unless they were shopping for broken pieces of glass.

I saw workmen running towards us, weaving their way through the rest of the traffic, which had come to a complete standstill. About half a dozen of them reached us at the same time and stood in a circle, staring, as if they didn't believe we were alive. I knew how they felt. I didn't quite believe it myself.

One of them pushed his way through. He was the site foreman ... at least, that's what it said on his badge. "Are you all right?" he gurgled. He didn't wait for an answer. Instead, he turned to his crew. "What the hell happened?"

Suddenly, everyone was shouting at each other, trying to pass the blame.

Then the crane operator arrived and instead of shouting at each other, the workmen all started shouting at him. He was a short, plump man and I could imagine him sitting in his little cabin all day, a hundred metres above the ground. He was wearing sunglasses but they were balanced crookedly on his nose. I almost felt sorry for him. He was close to tears.

"It wasn't my fault!" he wailed. "It was the computer! It went crazy. I didn't have any control. It was like the crane had a life of its own."

I don't remember very much more of what happened after that. Tim was standing beside me, chalk white, looking like the ghost he had almost become. I knew I probably looked the same. And just one thought was going through my mind. I was remembering the fortune cookies. *Drop the case or you will be violently murdered.*

We'd certainly been warned. And we hadn't had to wait very long.

Scary Bikers

We managed to get away from Cannon Street before the police arrived, which was probably just as well. I've probably been arrested more times than any fourteen-year-old in history. I even spent time in prison once.[2] And they'd want to ask me loads of questions when, right now, I had no answers. There was only one thing about the case I could say for sure: we should never have taken it on.

"Let's call Jane Nightingale," I said when we got back to the office. "I think it's time we met up with her again."

"You're right there, kid." Tim threw himself behind

---

2. See *Public Enemy Number Two*

the desk, not noticing that he'd left his chair in front of it. He disappeared from sight. "We should definitely be talking to her about a pay rise," he continued as he pulled himself back to his feet.

"How will money help us if we're both dead?"

Tim thought about it. "It'll pay for the funeral."

"I don't want a funeral, Tim. I like being alive. Even living with you!"

"What's so wrong with living with me?"

"The whole flat is falling down. There's no food in the fridge. We've only got a black-and-white TV!"

"Yes. But it's got four stations!"

"And two of them are weather channels!" I looked at him sadly. "Why do you always have to buy everything half price?"

"Because if I paid full price, it would cost me twice as much!"

I was about to argue but what was the point? I didn't want to upset Tim and I hadn't forgotten that if it weren't for him, I'd have nowhere to go. Apart from my brother, I had no living relatives in the UK. All four of my grandparents were in the same cemetery. In fact, to save money, they were all in the same grave. And it was too late to move in with my mum and dad. They were living in a small flat in Sydney with my baby sister and their new dog, Spotty. It wasn't a Dalmatian; it was just very sick. My dad was running his own business and it was really going places ... namely to the bankruptcy court. My mum had been forced to get a job as a waitress in a drive-through restaurant and she was finding it hard to lay the tables without getting run over. They'd both made it clear they had no time for me.

So if Tim threw me out now, who would have me? I'd probably end up in care. I'd be sent to an orphanage and all the other orphans would gang up on me because I actually had parents. No. I knew I had to stick around a little longer, which is why the two of us had come to an understanding. I understood Tim was a complete idiot. And he understood that without me he would never solve a single case. Somehow, we made it work.

Tim reached for the slip of paper with Jane

Nightingale's number and read it out. I made the call. There was a series of clicks but that was just Tim biting his nails. Then we were connected.

"This is Jane Nightingale." I recognized her voice ... warm and husky like a shaggy white dog in front of a fire. In a way I was surprised. I'd more or less decided that everything about her was fake. So why hadn't she given us a fake number too? "Have you had any luck finding my father?" she asked.

"Not yet," I said. And that was interesting. I hadn't said a word and she didn't have my telephone number. So how did she know who was calling? "We need to talk," I said.

"That's usually the reason people call."

"I don't mean on the phone," I said. "I think we should meet."

She didn't hesitate. "All right. Do you know Grannies?"

I did. Grannies was a fast-food restaurant in Kensington Road ... the other side of London. It served hamburgers in granary buns but that wasn't how it had got its name. All the staff were grandparents. In fact, they only employed people over the age of seventy-five. The whole idea was to show that even if you were very old, you could still have a job and be part of society. I wasn't so sure that the idea worked. A fast-food restaurant is fine ... but not when it takes an hour and a half for your food to arrive. And the staff weren't up to much. The chef didn't like the heat so he stayed out of the kitchen. The head waitress, Maisie, had been named employee of the month ... but that had been June 1973. The only real success was the ninety-year-old cocktail mixer. His hands shook so much that he was actually brilliant at his job.

We agreed to meet there for an early lunch and Jane Nightingale was waiting for us when we arrived. This time she was dressed for business with a black suede jacket and a little white cap that slanted across her head as if it was about to slide onto her shoulder. She seemed pleased to see us as we sat next to her at the table. For a moment, she rested a hand on Tim's knee and I got a brief glance of a tattoo, it looked like a lightning strike – on her wrist. Tim didn't notice anything. He was smiling so much he was showing all his teeth and several inches of gum.

"It's nice to see you, boys," she said. "Lunch is on me."

"Do you want me to get a cloth?" Tim asked.

She handed him the menu. "Choose what you want and I'll pay."

A waitress shuffled towards the table. She'd only come from the kitchen, but she was exhausted by the time she arrived. I watched as she took out a notepad and turned up her hearing aid. "Yes?" she asked.

"How's the spaghetti, Betty?" Tim said.

She scowled at him. "My name's Grace."

"Then I'll have the plaice."

Jane ordered a salad and I went for a burger. The Granny burger came with bacon, cheese and a gherkin, the whole thing held together by two miniature knitting needles. The waitress hobbled off and the three of us were left alone.

"So how are you getting on?" Jane asked.

"Not too well," I replied before Tim could speak.

"And maybe you should level with us, Ms Nightingale – if that's who you really are."

"What makes you think it's not?"

"Well, for a start, you don't know how to spell your father's name."

"I was never good at spelling. Sometimes I even get my own name wrong. Jayne. I put an extra letter in it."

"Y?" Tim asked.

"I just told you. Because I'm not very good at spelling."

"Why don't you tell us about Tommy and Troy?" I suggested.

"I can't tell you anything about them. I've never heard of them. They're complete strangers to me!"

"How do you know they're complete strangers if you've never met them?" Tim demanded.

"They came to the house in Bath while we were there," I explained. "They tried to kill us."

"They tried to kill you? That's terrible!"

"That's right," Tim said. "And it would have been even worse if they'd succeeded."

"So, what did they look like?"

I thought back. "Beards. Shaven heads. Broken noses. And guns. Everything about them was nasty, especially the guns. They were in the house looking for a rubber duck."

The description of the men had meant nothing to her but she sat up when she heard that. "A rubber duck? Is that what they said? Are you sure it wasn't a Rubber Ducky?"

"What's the difference?"

"A Rubber Ducky is a type of memory stick that you plug into a computer. It's a very powerful device."

"So how come I've never heard of it?" Tim asked.

"Have you heard of an Alfa Wi-Fi adapter, a key-logger, a Proxmark3 Kit?" Jane replied.

"What about them?" I said. She was wasting her time with Tim. He didn't even know what to do with a memory stick. Or if he had known once, he'd forgotten.

"They're all devices used by computer hackers," Jane replied.

"Is that what Alistair Nightingale is? A computer

hacker?" Thinking about the house, all the equipment we had seen, it made sense. "So what's your relationship with him?" I went on.

"I told you. I'm his daughter."

"I googled him and he doesn't have a daughter. He's never been married. He lives alone."

"I was adopted."

"Maybe. But not by him. I went into his house and it was obvious he's always lived alone. And there was something that didn't add up about that place too."

"Yes," Tim said, rubbing his nose. "Why did the letter box have such a strong spring?"

"How did he afford it? Bath is an expensive city. And you'd need a ton of money to live somewhere like the Royal Crescent. But Alistair Nightingale isn't exactly a successful author. *The Computer Code* sold a mere fifteen copies and *The Art of Algorithms* didn't even make double figures. His publishers only ever sent him on one author tour and that was just to get rid of him. They told him not to come back. His last book got a recommendation from Bill Gates. He recommended people not to buy it. So maybe you should tell us what's really going on here. Who is Alistair Nightingale and why are you looking for him?"

There was a long silence. One of the waitresses went past in a wheelchair pushed by another waitress. Finally, Jane nodded. "All right," she admitted. "I lied to you."

"I don't believe you!" Tim exclaimed.

"I'm not Alistair Nightingale's daughter, but I need to find him because I think he's in danger and I am too."

"Why?"

"OK. I'll explain..."

And I really think she might have, but just then there was an ugly throttling sound that came from outside. I looked through the window and saw two men in leather jackets, each on a Harley-Davidson motorbike – thick rubber tyres and gleaming chrome with raised handlebars and Union Jack flags fluttering behind. Even before the men had taken off their helmets, I knew who they were. You could say that the letters on their jackets – WC – had flushed them out.

"Tommy and Troy," I whispered. Somehow, they'd found us here. I watched them dismount their bikes. They were in no hurry.

Jane had seen them too. Her eyes widened. "You brought them here!" she snapped.

"No!" Tim protested. "They came on their bikes."

"They've followed you. We have to move..."

She was already getting up, edging out from behind the table. I went with her. There was only one door leading out of the restaurant and it would take us into the street – exactly where the two bikers were waiting. I noticed Tommy reach into his pocket and feel for something and I knew he wasn't about to check his phone for messages. Sure enough, the butt of a pistol appeared briefly in his hand. He was ready to shoot us down in broad daylight. I could already see it happening. A series of shots, the crowds scattering, the two men climbing back onto their bikes. They'd be on their way out of London long before the police arrived. And we'd be on the way to the morgue.

But Jane Nightingale wasn't leading us to the front door. Instead, we were weaving through the tables, heading for the kitchen, and, a moment later, we'd gone crashing through the swing doors into a world of white and silver, pots and pans hanging on hooks, bubbling sauces and sizzling meat. I could smell melting cheese and overcooked vegetables. The head chef was sitting in a corner, crying over his onion soup.

"We're looking for a back entrance," Jane announced.

"There isn't one," the chef said. "People who eat here don't usually come back."

"OK. How about a back exit?"

He pointed. "There's a fire door."

We took it, slamming it open and exiting into a narrow alley that ran along the side of the restaurant. Suddenly, we were the filling in a brick sandwich. There were walls on either side of us, looming up with no windows and just a few closed doors. We could turn left or we could turn right. It wasn't a great choice.

Jane moved away from Tim. "I think we should split up," she said.

"But we're not married!" Tim cried.

"We're safer if we go separate ways. I'll be in touch."

She might have had a point. Maybe we'd be less of a target if we separated. Or maybe she'd just decided she stood a better chance without us. After all, it was Tim and me that they were after. Tommy and Troy must have followed us from Bath, although I had no idea how they'd managed to track us down – not just to London but to a restaurant on the wrong side of town. Anyway, they were going to finish the job they'd started and this time they weren't going to let a pussy cat get in the way. We were in serious trouble.

Jane had turned left and was already in the distance, disappearing from sight. We went the other way, but even as we came out of the alleyway, I knew we'd made the wrong choice. We were back in Kensington Road. Tommy and Troy's motorbikes were parked in front of the restaurant.

And so were Tommy and Troy. We hadn't taken two steps before we were seen.

"There they are!" I heard Troy call out. "Let's get them!"

The two men pulled their helmets back on. It took Tommy a moment longer because he'd put his on back to front. But then they climbed onto their motorbikes and revved up the engines. They weren't going to run after us ... their legs were more suited to waddling.

But they had motorbikes that could cover a hundred metres in five seconds flat. And it would only take them six seconds going uphill.

Worse still, they weren't alone. We had already started running across the road when I heard the same throaty roar of more motorbikes arriving, and sure enough two more bikers with dark glasses, sprouting beards and fluttering Union Jacks turned the corner and ploughed through the traffic, heading towards us. They clearly went to the same tailor as Tommy and Troy. They wore the same black leather jackets and dirty jeans and I could imagine the letters "WC" set out in silver studs on their backs, even though I couldn't see them. Both of them had stomachs that bulged out almost to their knees. There'd be no point in them weighing themselves on a bathroom scale. They wouldn't be able to see it.

Four motorbikes in the streets of Kensington. It was obvious that we had to get inside. Any building would be safe: a shop, an office, a department store. Perhaps somewhere with a basement where we could hide.

Anywhere where four thugs on motorbikes couldn't follow us.

"This way!" Tim shouted.

"No!" I cried. But it was too late. He had run into a multistorey car park.

I had no choice. I couldn't leave him on his own. Even though I knew I was signing my own death warrant, I followed him up a ramp and into the gloomy interior. There were hardly any cars parked here but that was because of the price. You could probably spend a week in the Costa Brava for the same cost as a couple of hours in a Kensington car park. Leave your car here and you'd have to sell it to pay the exit fee. As we ran up to the second floor and then the third, all I could see was a grey concrete emptiness that stretched out in all directions, with more ramps climbing up and down and solid pillars separating the different bays. For about half a second I wondered if Tommy and Troy had managed to miss us going in. Then I heard the roar of engines behind us and I knew they had seen us. They were gleefully following us and we had nowhere to hide.

Could there be anything worse than being cornered by four crazy armed bikers in the middle of London? Yes. As we fled across the deserted third floor, I realized that there were now six of them. Two more had arrived, entering the car park from somewhere on the other side. The echo of their engines was all around us and I could smell the petrol fumes pushing out whatever fresh air had managed to linger inside. The bikers hadn't found us yet. From the sound of the engines, they were buzzing around on the floor below us. But it was only a matter of time. Desperately, I looked for a staircase. Our only hope was to get back into the street. The sides of the car park had narrow slits that allowed in a little daylight, but looking out I saw that our situation was even worse than I'd thought. There were yet more bikers outside, circling the building. Whichever way we went, we were trapped.

I saw a door marked "EXIT". Was it referring to the car park or to my life? It didn't matter. Coming in here had been a mistake and our only hope was to get back out again and take our chances among the traffic.

Anyway, there was something undignified about being splattered across the third floor of a multistorey car park, particularly since I didn't even have a car. I preferred to die in the sunshine. The door was a long way away. Did we have time to reach it?

We didn't. Before I'd taken another step, one of the bikers appeared, cruising up the ramp and emerging like some black-and-silver monster rising from the grave. He had no face ... just a beard and dark glasses beneath a black helmet. He looked straight at me. I saw him mutter a few words and realized that he was wearing a throat mic. That was how he was keeping in touch with the others. He stayed where he was, waiting for them to join him. The door was in front of us.

"Move, Tim!"

We began to run and I heard the motorbike revving up behind us. There was almost no hope. The door was too far away. Maybe the biker would get a puncture. Maybe he'd slip on a puddle of oil and break his neck. Maybe a meteor from outer space would crash down and obliterate him. I guessed that all three of these possibilities were about as likely as each other, but what was certain was that, without a miracle, he would cut us off in seconds. His friends were already on their way. I could hear them accelerating on the floor below. The whole car park seemed to be trembling. Tim definitely was. The door still seemed like a mile away.

And then it happened. There was a screech of tyres, rubber burning on concrete, and a car came shooting out of nowhere – a silver BMW with tinted windows. It raced across the concrete floor, heading for us so fast that for an instant I thought it was going to run us over. But at the last moment, it swerved round, smoke rising underneath it, and stopped. The back door flew open. "Get in!" a voice demanded.

It wasn't Jane Nightingale. It was a man in his thirties with the sort of face that had seen a lot of trouble and maybe caused even more. He had hard brown eyes and thin lips that barely covered his teeth. "Move it!" he rasped.

"Wait a minute," Tim said. "We didn't order an Uber—"

"Just do it, Tim!" I shouted.

The biker was hesitating, some distance away. But two more bikes had arrived behind him. Tommy and Troy. They had their guns out, balanced on their handlebars. I pushed Tim into the car and threw myself on top of him. The driver took off without bothering to wait for us to close the door but somehow, I managed to reach out and pull it shut. The car swerved, heading towards the down ramp, the tyres screaming as they gripped the corners. A fourth biker accelerated out of our way. By now he must have realized that our driver – whoever he was – didn't intend to stop and ask for directions.

We continued down two more levels, then burst out into the open. I saw more bikers in the road behind us, but they were facing in the wrong direction and didn't know what had happened. And then we were away, moving more slowly now, joining the traffic on the high street.

"Thank you," I said.

"You can drop us off at the station," Tim added.

"Shut up and stay still!" The driver pressed a button and I heard the doors lock automatically.

I settled back in the soft leather and decided to enjoy the view of Hyde Park as we drove past. All in all, there wasn't much else I could do.

Old Friends

The silver BMW took us across London. We were stuck in the back. The doors were locked. And to make matters worse, the driver had produced a massive gun of his own: five pounds of steel loaded with six ounces of lead. He slipped it into a holster under his jacket but only after making sure we'd seen it. The message was clear: *I'm in charge and if you disagree, make sure you've written your will.* As we joined the traffic on Oxford Street, I tried starting a conversation.

"Where are you taking us?" I asked.

"You'll find out," the man growled. He would have made a great ventriloquist. When he talked, his lips hardly moved.

Tim leaned forward. "And when will that be?" he demanded.

The driver grunted. "Keep asking questions and the only place you'll be going is the cemetery."

"Sure," I muttered. "Drop us at St Michael's in Camden and we can walk the rest of the way home."

He wasn't amused. In fact, he nearly knocked over a cyclist as he swung round at a traffic light and headed towards Clerkenwell. As we continued through Holborn, leaving the busiest part of the city behind us, I suddenly got the feeling that I knew where we were going. There had been something familiar about the driver from the start. I'd never met him before but I sort of recognized him: the suit, the gun and the expressionless face. Sure enough, he turned into a shabby-looking dead end behind the meat market and I saw a sign: KELLY STREET. That was when I knew I was right.

"We've been here before," I muttered to Tim.

Tim shook his head. "You're wrong, kid," he replied. "I've never been in this car in my life."

"Not the car, Tim. The street!" The vehicle slowed down and stopped outside number seventeen. "Now do you remember?" I asked. "When we were chasing after Charon, we were given knock-out gas in the back of a cab!"[3]

Tim stared at me. "That's terrible. I hope we didn't leave a tip!"

"And we were brought here to meet the head of MI6."

"I remember now. Mr Crazily!"

"That's right, Tim. Except his name was Waverly."

"So why have we come back?"

"I don't know. I expect we'll find out."

OK. If you haven't read *South by South East*, let me give you a quick rundown. Number seventeen was a narrow building with four storeys and an ugly glass door. It looked empty and abandoned but, actually, it was the headquarters of MI6 – in other words, the secret service. Mr Waverly was the boss of MI6 and he had forced us to help him find an international assassin

---

3   See *South by South East*

known as Charon. We'd found Charon. We'd almost got killed. Somehow we'd survived. That's all you need to know. And now you don't need to buy the book.

We got out of the car and stood on the pavement in the warm afternoon air. If I'd had the chance, I'd have made a run for it, but the driver was right behind us and I hadn't forgotten about the gun under his jacket.

"Don't do anything stupid!" he warned us.

That was going to be a tough call for Tim.

The front door opened automatically and he led us down a bare concrete corridor to a blank wall with a fire extinguisher hanging in the middle. I knew what was going to come next. The fire extinguisher was fake. The driver turned a nozzle and the whole wall swung open to reveal modern offices full of computers, with young, smartly dressed men and women making their way silently across grey-coloured carpets. It was a neat trick, although I still wondered what they'd do if there was a fire.

We continued into an office where Mr Waverly was waiting for us. Not a lot had changed since the last time we were here. He was even wearing the same three-piece suit and the same old school tie – Eton or Harrow, or wherever he'd done his GCSEs in history, maths and espionage. He was about seventy years old, a very serious-looking man with greying hair and greying eyes, sitting behind a desk with his fingers crossed like a professor ... or someone who's been playing with a tube of superglue.

He was not alone. A woman was perched on a chair to one side and even before Tim and I had entered the room, I could see that she had taken a dislike to us, which was fast work. Normally, people at least waited until Tim had said a few words. She looked like a head teacher, with a narrow face, glasses and silver hair that had been cut using scissors and a ruler. She was wearing a tight-fitting jacket and skirt, thick stockings and black leather shoes with long, pointed heels that could easily stab a man to death. She examined us with small, hostile eyes as if all her worst fears had just been realized. She didn't smile. I got the feeling she didn't know how to.

"Please sit down," Mr Waverly said. There were two

seats in front of the desk. We took them. He glanced at the man who had brought us here. "You can leave us, Flint. Thank you."

"Flint?" I watched as the driver left. "What happened to Ed, Ted and Red?"

Those had been the names of the agents who had brought us here last time.

"I'm afraid Ed and Ted have left the service," Waverly explained.

"And Red?"

"Red is dead."

"That's too bad," I said. "Shame his name wasn't Burt."

"And why is that?"

"He might just have been hurt."

The woman with the killer heels didn't find that funny. "What are these two doing here?" she asked. *These two.* She made us sound like something the cat had dragged in. "They're an obvious security risk."

"They've helped us before," Waverly said. "Mr Diamond here is a quite remarkable private detective."

Remarkably bad? Remarkably useless? He didn't say.

"His brother is also a very bright boy," he added.

That was me.

The woman didn't agree. "I hope you're not suggesting that he can be of any use to us," she continued. "The idea of a fourteen-year-old boy working for the secret service is the most stupid thing I've ever heard—"

"Wait a minute," I cut in. "Why don't you explain what's going on around here? Were you the ones who sent us those messages in the fortune cookies? And what was 'Flint' doing in Kensington just now? It was quite a coincidence him turning up just like that."

Waverly looked straight at me. "I don't believe in coincidences," he said.

Tim's eyes brightened. "That's a coincidence!" he exclaimed. "Neither do I!"

"I think you should get these two out of here," the woman said. "We have work to do."

"Allow me to introduce you," Waverly said. "This is Fiona Duncan-Jones. She is the new chief of MI6. Very

soon this office will be hers. I'm very sorry to say that I've been asked to retire. I just have one last operation."

"You're not well?" Tim asked.

"I'm referring to the operation which you and your brother have managed to involve yourselves in: the White Crusaders and the kidnapping of Alistair Nightingale."

White Crusaders. WC. I remembered the studs I had seen on the jackets of Tommy and Troy, and at least one part of the jigsaw fell into place.

"Why don't you tell us what's going on, Mr Waverly?" I asked. "And this time, please don't knock us out when you've finished with us." That was what had happened the last time we were here. He'd given us a drink and we'd woken up back in Camden. "We can walk out on our own two feet."

"Four feet," Tim said. "We've got two each."

"This is a waste of time!" Fiona growled.

"No, no. On the contrary. I think the Diamond brothers might be very helpful to us." I could see Waverly making his calculations. He was the sort of man who knew exactly what he was going to say a week before he said it. "Everything I'm about to tell you is top secret," he began.

"Then why are you telling us?" Tim said.

"Because you need to know. But you mustn't tell anyone else."

"Don't worry, Mr Heavily. Your secrets are as safe with me as the PIN code of my bank card." He turned to Fiona. "It's 2233, by the way."

"All right. Let's start at the beginning and that

means the White Crusaders. They're the gentlemen on the motorbikes who almost killed you in Bath and who tracked you down in Kensington. Not very pleasant people, I'm sure you'll agree."

"They were certainly no gentlemen," I said.

"The White Crusaders are an extremely nasty political organization. You may have noticed the Union Jacks on their motorbikes. They want to make Britain great again – that's their slogan – but they believe the best way to do that is to go fifty years into the past. They hate foreigners and they'd love to start another world war because they're convinced they would win. Even if they lost, they'd be happy, as long as they could kill lots of foreigners. Basically, they're completely mad but they're well organized and they have a lot of powerful people behind them – and that makes them unusually dangerous.

"Their leader is a man called Neville Fairfax. When he was a teenager, his parents were killed in a car accident. They were run over by a French driver in an Italian car on a German road. They were rushed to a Belgian hospital but the Swiss doctor couldn't save them. This may be the reason why he hates foreigners. His father was actually a baron. Neville was his only son and inherited all his money as well as the family home.

"That home happens to be a small island in the North Sea. For the last five hundred years, the Fairfaxes have owned Hare Island, about a mile and a half east of Aberdeen. What you have to understand is that although it's part of the UK, Hare Island is an independent state. Fairfax is the Chief Minister and the island has its own laws and taxes. Six hundred people live there. All of this is very important to what I'm going to tell you.

"Fairfax would very much like to be the leader, not just of a small island, but the whole of the UK. We've been watching him for some time and recently we discovered that he'd come up with a plan to achieve just that. What he and his people want to do is to break into the GCHQ computer system in Cheltenham. GCHQ stands for Government Communications Headquarters. It's the country's most important security centre, providing vital information to the government and to the police. If Fairfax managed to get access to their computers, can you imagine what the result would be?"

"No!" Tim said. "I can't!"

"Well, it would be a complete nightmare. He'd be in total control of the armed forces as well as the secret service, including MI5 and MI6. He would be able to operate our nuclear missiles. He would know everything about everyone in the country. If he could hack into the government computers, he could do almost anything he wanted. With a flick of a switch, he could shut down the NHS or close all the airports. He would have unlimited power."

"But that's impossible," I said. I noticed Fiona Duncan-Jones giving me an ugly look but I went on anyway. "Nobody could break into the government's computers. It would be too difficult."

"That's what we thought," Waverly agreed. "But we were wrong. There is just one man in the world, a super hacker, a technical genius who has already broken into computer systems in the Kremlin, the Pentagon, the special weapons facilities in North Korea – as well as Apple, Microsoft and Amazon. Of course, he doesn't use his own name. We know him only as zEbra. Small Z, big E. He lives completely off-grid and there are many people who believe he doesn't even exist. But recently, we managed to track him down..."

"Alistair Nightingale," I said. I remembered the odd details I had seen in his house. The stuffed toy zebra in the bedroom. The zebra-skin rug downstairs. The picture of a zebra crossing in the library. "So Alistair Nightingale is zEbra!" I said.

But even as I spoke the words, I was certain something was wrong. Nightingale was an author, in his fifties. He lived in a nice house in Bath. Nothing about him fitted the profile of a major computer hacker.

But Waverly nodded. "That's exactly right. Alistair Nightingale is zEbra," he said. "He's written books on computers but that's just a front for his real activities. We believe he has fifty million pounds tucked away in the bank – most of it in bitcoin."

"What's bitcoin?" Tim asked.

"It's a cryptocurrency," I said.

"Right. And what's a cryptocurrency?"

"It's like electronic money, Tim. You can use it without needing a bank."

Fortunately, Tim knew what a bank was.

"The White Crusaders have kidnapped zEbra and he's being held prisoner in a castle on Hare Island. We believe they're going to force him to hack into the government computers. Perhaps they're going to torture him."

Well, they could have given him my maths homework for starters, I thought. But I didn't say that. Instead, I asked, "If you know where he is, why don't you go in and rescue him?"

"We'll come to that in a moment," Waverly replied. He turned to Tim. "The first thing we want to know is what were you and your little brother doing in the Royal Crescent?"

Tim leaned forward. "That's our business," he muttered.

"If you don't want to cooperate, we can lock you up downstairs until this operation is over," said Fiona

Duncan-Jones. "How do you fancy a month in solitary confinement?"

"It'll be fine as long as we're not alone," Tim said.

I was liking Fiona less and less, and I hadn't exactly taken to her in the first place. "All right," I said. "We were looking for Alistair Nightingale. We were asked to find him by his daughter, Jane. She told us she was worried about him and she thought he might have been kidnapped."

Waverly frowned. "Alistair Nightingale doesn't have a daughter," he said.

"We'd already worked that out for ourselves," I replied. "We knew she was a fake. That's why we went to meet her at Grannies."

The two spies exchanged a glance. "We have no record of any Jane Nightingale," Waverly said. "Can you describe her?"

"She's gorgeous—" Tim said.

"Blonde hair, blue eyes, slim, about twenty-five years old," I cut in. "We can't tell you anything more. We've only met her twice. So why don't you answer some of our questions, Mr Waverly? Did you send us the messages with the fortune cookies?"

He nodded. "Yes. I was trying to warn you off."

"And how did you know we'd be at Grannies?"

"We've been watching you for some time now ... luckily for you. If Flint hadn't turned up when he did, you'd be finished."

"We're finished anyway," I said. "This has got nothing to do with us. Jane Nightingale – or whoever she is – lied to us. You know where to find zEbra. You don't need us!" I got to my feet.

"Sit down!" Fiona snapped.

And "snapped" was exactly the right word. I'd met crocodiles who were friendlier than her.

"Let me explain our situation to you," Waverly went on. He sounded completely reasonable. Like a vicar offering you a cup of tea. "We cannot storm onto Hare Island and rescue zEbra. As I told you, it's not exactly part of the UK. So right now, we're putting together a top-secret mission. We're planning to send in a small team of professionals to extract Nightingale. But even that won't be easy. The castle where he is being held is called Seagull's Rise. It's at the top of a mountain and can only be reached by a cable car that climbs up and down from the main town.

"To make matters worse, everyone who lives on Hare Island has the same views as Neville Fairfax. They're all fanatics. There'll be armed guards everywhere. It's not only legal to carry a gun on Hare Island, it's compulsory. Nobody is allowed to visit the island without a visa. There's only one ferry a week from the mainland and no one's allowed on – not even the captain – until they've been thoroughly checked.

"Our team will have to go in by canoe from the coast of Scotland. They'll paddle to the island and break into Seagull's Rise. They'll have to locate zEbra, get him out of the castle and somehow make it to the other side of the island without being killed. A helicopter will be standing by to pick them up."

"It all sounds thrilling," I said. "But what's it got to do with us?"

"Right now, the two of you are a security risk. We could hold you here until the operation is over but it seems to me more sensible to send you in with our team. As a matter of fact, you could be exactly what we need."

There was something nasty about the way he said that. But Waverly was the sort of man who could make "Good morning!" sound like a death threat.

"What do you mean?" I asked.

"Let's just say that you have certain skills that could be useful to us."

That didn't make any sense either. "What skills are you talking about, Mr Waverly?" Tim was just about up to tying his own shoelaces and he'd recently taken a night course in flower arranging, but I didn't see how either of those things were going to help us climb a mountain and break into a castle filled with maniacs with machine guns.

"We don't need to go into that," Waverly said. "You'll get a full briefing when you arrive in Gargle."

"Where's Gargle?"

"It's a fishing village two miles from Aberdeen. It used to be three miles from Aberdeen but there's been a lot of coastal erosion. Flint will tell you everything you need to know."

Tim looked around him. "Flint isn't here," he said.

"He'll tell you everything you need to know when you get there," Waverly explained.

"But will he tell us how to get there?" Tim asked. "Because that's the first thing we need to know."

"Oh, for heaven's sake!" Fiona snapped, her eyes colder than ever. "This guy is a complete and utter idiot!"

"That's not a nice thing to say about Mr Lovely," Tim said.

"I'm not talking about Mr Waverly. I'm talking about you!" Fiona turned to her boss. "Are you really sure we need them?"

Waverly nodded. "Appearances can be deceptive," he said. "But let me assure you that Tim Diamond and his brother have a unique way of doing things. I think it may turn out that we're very lucky they've shown up a second time."

"Wait a minute!" I shook my head in disbelief. "We haven't actually agreed to any of this. What makes you think either of us wants to volunteer for this crazy mission?"

"Of course, it's entirely your decision." Waverly smiled. "You can stay in London and wait for the White Crusaders to find you again. Next time, I'm sure they'll turn you into mincemeat and we won't be there to pick up the pieces."

Mincemeat. That was a lot of pieces.

"Or you can join us and we'll look after you. You may even get a medal. That's what it comes down to. You're with us or you're on your own. Which is it to be?"

A Nasty Development

"I don't understand!" Tim exclaimed. "Why didn't you say yes?"

I stared at him. "Are you serious?" I replied. "You really wanted to join in Mr Waverly's suicide mission?"

"There's nothing wrong with a suicide mission, provided you don't get killed..."

"Tim..." I had to take a deep breath. "Try to get this into your head. The only reason he asked us to go to Hare Island was because he wanted to use us. I don't know what's going on in *his* head but whatever it is, it's not going to be good for our health. Don't you remember what happened last time? He turned us into bait.

He wanted Charon to kill us because it would help him find out who Charon was. He didn't care if we lived or died."

"But he said we had specialist skills!"

"This case has already become too dangerous." I shook my head. "The White Crusaders have tried to kill us twice and someone dropped a steel girder on us."

"That may have been an accident."

"Well, we've had enough accidents. We're going to keep our heads down for the next few weeks. And from now on, I think you should only take on easy cases. Like finding a missing dog, for example."

Tim sighed. "The last time I found a missing dog, it bit me." He thought for a moment. "So did the owner!"

We were back at the flat in Camden Town. It would have been about teatime if we'd had any tea. After I'd told Waverly that, thank you very much, I'd prefer not to take a canoe ride across the North Sea to storm an island full of fanatics and rescue a genius computer hacker I'd never met, he'd been surprisingly pleasant, even offering us a lift home. I'd thanked him but declined. The trouble with Waverly was that when he sent a car for you, you couldn't be sure if it would pick you up or run you over. We'd taken a bus.

Tim wasn't happy. Maybe it was the knowledge that Jane Nightingale had lied to him. He'd fallen for her the moment she'd glided into the office, but she'd used him. I almost felt sorry for him. Tim had never been very lucky in love. His first girlfriend was a trapeze artist but she dropped him. Since then, there had hardly been any girls in his life ... not until Jane Nightingale had walked into the room and walked straight back out again. Was Jane even her name? I had no idea who she really was or why she'd contacted us. I remembered how quickly she had abandoned us at Grannies.

Tim had left his laptop open on the desk and suddenly it pinged as a message popped up. I glanced at the screen. To my surprise, it was actually from Jane.

> Hi, Tim. Sorry to run out on you at that restaurant. I was going to tell you the truth about me. There are lots of things you need

to know. Meet me tonight. I'll be
at Battersea Tower in Battersea
Bridge Road at 8 p.m. It's a new
office development and we can
meet there safely. Come to the
29th floor. Jane xxx

I read it quickly. The message was only a few lines
long but none of it made any sense. First of all, how
come she knew Tim's email address? He hadn't given
it to her. Second, how could she be so sure that we had
escaped from Grannies? We could have been captured
or shot, but she hadn't even asked where we were. And
here was the biggest question of all: why did she want
to meet us at an office development in South London?
That was crazy. We'd be just as safe in a café or a pub
round the corner. I didn't like anything about Jane
Nightingale. I'd only met her twice but she'd been
nothing but trouble.

Tim didn't agree. He pointed at the screen. "Oh,
look! She's sent me three kisses!"

"It's probably a typing error," I growled. "I think

there are some questions we need to ask about this message."

"Yeah." Tim nodded. "Battersea Tower in Battersea Bridge Road. Where do you think that is?"

"It could be in Battersea," I suggested.

"You might be right. Do you think she works there?"

"I don't know. But I don't think we should go."

"Why not?"

"Because it might be a trap."

"We won't know until we walk into it."

"Which is exactly why we shouldn't go."

Tim gave me a crooked smile. "Don't worry, kid. I'll look after you."

"That's what worries me."

There was no arguing with Tim. We went.

There's so much new building in Battersea that even the pigeons wear hard hats. Everywhere you look, there are cranes and scaffolding, cement mixers, diggers and mountains of bricks that go down as fast as the flats and offices go up. Walk from one end to the other and by the time you get there you won't be able to find your way back.

Battersea Tower was in the middle of it all. It was about thirty storeys high and somehow managed to be completely different and yet exactly the same as all the buildings around it. There was a courtyard with a fountain and a curving entrance with doors that were five times as big as they needed to be. Great glass windows like oversized playing cards had been piled up on one another, held together in an ugly steel and concrete frame. There were very few lights on inside. It was eight o'clock and everyone would have gone home after work, but I got the feeling that nobody actually worked here yet. It was a brand-new development and it didn't have any sense of life. Even the fountain was dry.

We walked up to the entrance, our footsteps rapping on the concrete. The sun had set but the evening air was still warm. I was quite sure that the journey across London had been a waste of time. For some reason, Jane Nightingale had lured us to an office building that still hadn't opened and there was no way we were going to get in. And although I could see a reception desk that seemed to stretch on for a mile in each direction, there was nobody sitting behind it. The whole place felt empty. But there was some movement. As we got closer to the doors, I noticed a CCTV camera blink with a single red eye and twist round to follow us. It unnerved me. It reminded me of the cameras at Nightingale's house in the Royal Crescent. Why did I get the feeling that it was the same person watching me? Worse still, I had no idea who they were.

We reached the doors and they slid open immediately, making no sound at all.

"Hello?" Tim called out.

Nobody answered. There was no one there.

We stepped inside the reception area. For a moment, we stood in front of the empty desk, staring at a blank wall with no pictures, no company names. It confirmed my suspicion that the building was unoccupied.

"I don't like it..." I muttered.

"I think it's quite nice," Tim disagreed. "It just needs a bit of decoration..."

"I'm not talking about the decor, Tim. I just mean ... it's too quiet."

The doors closed behind us, again without a sound. There was just a faint *click* of glass meeting glass and I wondered if they would open again to let us leave. I decided to find out. I retraced my steps, holding out a hand to trigger the infrared beam or whatever sensor would activate them.

Nothing happened.

We were stuck. We'd just walked into the trap that I'd been fearing all along.

"What now?" I whispered.

I was talking to myself but Tim answered. "The email said she'd meet us on the nineteenth floor," he said.

"The twenty-ninth," I corrected him.

Either way, it was a lot of stairs.

I'd noticed five gleaming silver lift doors on the far side of the lobby and had wondered if they were working. But even as I spoke, the one in the middle slid open.

It was almost as if it had read my mind. I was getting more and more spooked out with every minute that passed. As we walked towards the lifts, I heard a soft whirring and noticed another camera swivel in our direction. Everything was weird. It was as if the building itself was watching us, as if it had invited us in from the beginning and was now telling us where to go. Given a choice, I'd have headed right back out again. But I didn't have a choice. The front doors wouldn't let me.

We stepped into the lift. There were buttons numbered one to thirty-three but I didn't press any of them. I didn't need to. The doors closed and with incredible speed the lift whisked us upwards. Like the glass entrance doors, it made no sound. I only knew we were moving because of the flickering numbers in the display panel and the strange feeling in my stomach as it sank towards the ground.

We arrived at the twenty-ninth floor. The doors slid open, releasing us.

Somehow the lift had known where we wanted to go.

We walked into a modern office space that was

almost the size of a football pitch with dozens of desks, computers, sofas, lights, filing cabinets, telephones, potted plants, coffee machines ... everything you'd expect, apart from people eating crisps and dozing in their chairs. There was no sign of Jane Nightingale but I was fairly certain she wasn't going to show up. We were on our own.

"This is a bad idea, Tim," I whispered. In this building, even the fire extinguishers could have been listening in on us. "We shouldn't have come."

"There doesn't seem to be anyone here," Tim agreed.

I went over to the nearest desk and picked up a telephone, held it against my ear. "It's dead," I muttered. I took out my own phone and glanced at the screen. "No signal."

"There's no need to panic," Tim said. It was what he always said when he was about to panic.

"Let's just get out of here."

I hit the lift button. There might have been a staircase out of there but I didn't fancy walking twenty-nine floors. We watched the light blink on the display panel as the lift made its way up to us, and all the time I knew that it wasn't going to be as easy as this, that we weren't out of trouble yet. The lift doors slid open.

Tim looked at me. "You see?" he said. "Nothing to worry about."

He moved forward and, seeing what was about to happen, I threw myself at him and just managed to grab hold of him before he took the single step that would have killed him.

"What are you doing?" Tim shrieked. "I thought you wanted to leave."

"Take a look, Tim," I exclaimed.

Somehow the whole system had been repro-grammed. We'd called the lift. The display had shown it was coming. But when the doors had opened, there was nothing there. Instead, I was looking into an empty lift shaft with a dark tunnel of death between us and the ground, twenty-nine storeys below.

"The lift isn't there," I said.

Tim stared. "You're right!" he exclaimed. He thought for a moment. "It's been stolen!"

"No, it hasn't, Tim. Someone is trying to kill us."

"You think this happened on purpose?"

"Of course it did. They wanted us to step into the empty lift shaft."

"Who'd be stupid enough to do that?"

I didn't want to remind him that if I hadn't grabbed hold of him, he'd have reached the bottom floor a whole lot quicker than he'd intended.

"What are we going to do?" Tim asked. His eyes brightened. "Maybe we should try a different lift."

"I'm not getting in any lift, Tim. It's too dangerous. There must be a set of emergency stairs."

I looked around.

From where I was standing, I could see the entire twenty-ninth floor, with grey carpet and neon lights stretching into the distance. It wasn't exactly open-plan. There were corridors, different-sized offices, meeting areas and kitchens. But they were mainly separated by glass panels so that you could see through them from one to another. Everything was hi-tech. The lights and air conditioning must have been controlled by some central computer because I couldn't see any switches. You know those old mirror mazes you get at funfairs? It was a bit like that but without the fun.

I noticed an exit sign, glowing red on the far side, about two hundred metres away. That was the way out of the maze.

We began to move towards it, one step at a time. If a lift door could open without a lift, who could say what Battersea Tower might throw at us? Treading carefully, we followed a central corridor with offices on both sides, all the time keeping our eyes fixed on the emergency exit. But we'd hardly taken ten steps before there was a soft *hiss* and a glass door suddenly slid in front of us, blocking the way.

"A glass door has slid in front of us, blocking the way," Tim said.

"Yes, Tim. I know."

With the corridor ahead now closed off, we had a choice between left and right. What difference would it make which way we went? I turned right. We'd only taken two more steps before another door slid shut behind us.

"Hey, Nick, another..."

"I know, Tim. Don't tell me."

There was no going back.

It was a cat-and-mouse game, except that we were the mice and there was no sign of the cat. I looked up and saw a CCTV camera trained on us and wondered who it was, watching us on the monitor, flicking the switches. Jane Nightingale? That was the obvious answer. She was the one who had summoned us here. But it suddenly occurred to me that we had no proof that she'd sent us the email in the first place. Anyone could have hacked into Tim's computer – and, after all, we were dealing with zEbra, who according to Waverly was the greatest computer hacker in the world.

All the lights went out.

It was only eight thirty in the evening but the sun had slipped behind the building and the shadows rushed in. Standing in the gloom, I noticed that a single light had come on in an office down the end of another corridor. Without really thinking, we made our way towards it. What else could we do? It seemed to be telling us that maybe this way was safe.

We arrived in a cubicle with three glass walls and one solid one. It was empty apart from a desk and a chair, with a single light fitting mounted on the brickwork and a smoke alarm in the middle of the ceiling. There was another door, which I thought might lead somewhere, but when I opened it, I found myself looking into a cupboard full of envelopes and notepads. "It's stationery," I said.

"Yeah," Tim agreed. "It's not going anywhere. So what now?"

"We're going to have to go back the way we came."

But there was no way back. As we'd entered the room, yet another glass door had slid across the opening, locking us in. We were trapped in a small square office. Maybe it had been designed for a junior secretary or an intern – someone who wouldn't complain that they were being treated like a hamster. I still had no idea what was going on. We had been led here deliberately. Now we were stuck. But why? What was the big idea?

That was when the sprinkler system came to life, showering us with cold water from the ceiling. Every office building in the world has a sprinkler system in case of fire, but this one had only been activated in the space in which we found ourselves. Looking through the glass partitions, I could see that the rest of the floor was dry.

The water was coming down in a rush and in seconds we were drenched. My first thought was that this was all some insane practical joke. We'd been brought here to be soaked and that was the end of it. Tim was staring at the ceiling as if he still hadn't quite worked out what was going on. But I'd guessed. With a nasty feeling in my stomach, I realized that the office was completely watertight. With nowhere to go, the water was rising quite rapidly. Already it was lapping at my ankles. Remorselessly, it moved up to my calves.

It was completely crazy but in about five minutes it would reach the ceiling. Tim and I were about to be drowned, indoors, on the twenty-ninth floor of a state-of-the-art office development ... a nasty development in every sense. Actually, there was a good chance that we wouldn't drown. We might be electrocuted first. If the water reached the light fitting and it short-circuited, we'd be in for a shock – and it wasn't one we'd be likely to survive.

The water was still being sprayed all around us, splashing down and rising up the walls. It was like standing in a swimming pool in the rain. I'd thought it would take five minutes to fill the office space, but at this rate it was going to be a lot less.

"My knees are getting wet!" Tim exclaimed.

"I know, Tim," I said.

There was a pause and then: "My tummy's getting wet!"

That was how fast the water was moving.

I looked for something – anything – that I could use to break the glass. I waded across the carpet and picked up the office chair, then smashed it into the nearest wall. It didn't work. The glass was inches thick and reinforced. I couldn't even scratch it. Maybe it would be possible to use the desk as a battering ram? I tried moving it but it was too heavy. I pulled open the drawers. I don't know what I hoped to find inside – a fire axe seemed unlikely, but you never know. In fact, there was nothing that could help. Some pencils, plastic files, paper, an *A–Z* of London, half a packet of digestive biscuits.

The water had reached my stomach too. And it was continuing its journey towards my armpits.

"What are we going to do?" Tim shouted.

"I don't know!" I shouted back.

"We could call the police."

"I don't have a signal!"

The water was coming down even harder. I felt its grip, cold, around my ribs. A wastepaper basket that I hadn't noticed bobbed up and floated past. The water was sloshing against the glass walls. The rest of the office, still dark, had disappeared.

But just for once Tim had given me an idea. We couldn't call the police – but what about the fire brigade? I glanced at the light fitting, then the smoke alarm, finally the desk. Maybe there was something inside that I could use after all. I pulled open the

drawer and grabbed a file and two sheets of paper.

"Help me with the desk!" I shouted.

"What do you want to do with it?"

"I want to move it."

"I think it's nice where it is..."

I scowled at Tim and he came over and helped. Between us, we were just able to drag the desk so that one end was under the light and the other under the smoke alarm. I climbed on top. The light fitting was modern, steel and plastic jutting out of the wall. I was nervous about electrocuting myself but I couldn't see any other way. I grabbed hold of the metal base and, with all my strength, wrenched it out of the wall. The light flickered and went out.

"What did you do that for?" Tim's voice came out of the gloom.

"You'll see, Tim."

"I can't see anything! You've broken the light!"

The desk moved under my feet. The water had risen so far up that even a piece of furniture weighing half a ton was about to float away. "Hold the desk for me, Tim!" I called out. At the same time, I felt with my fingers, separating the two electric wires that had been left dangling. The water was rising faster than ever. It had begun creeping over my ankles again, even though I was standing high up on the desk. I heard Tim splashing around beneath me. Carefully, I extracted one of the sheets of paper I'd found, using the plastic file as a cover to keep it dry. Then I pressed the paper against the two ends of wire, at the same time thanking Mr Perkins, my physics teacher, who had assured me only a few weeks before that paper does not conduct electricity. Aren't teachers wonderful? The two wires came into contact with each other and sparked. Exactly as I hoped, the spark set fire to the paper. I waited until it was well alight, then lifted it up and pressed it against the smoke detector.

The water hammered against the flame and a few seconds later it went out – but not before it had done the trick. The smoke alarm activated and a siren went off all over the building. The entire sprinkler system came into operation and water began to shower down all over the twenty-ninth floor, which might not seem all that helpful ... but, actually, it saved our lives. All the pressure had been on the one little room where we were trapped. That was why it had filled up so quickly. But with twenty more sprinklers in operation, the water was spread out all over the office and the downpour turned into something closer to a drizzle.

As I climbed down from the desk, I saw something else. Like many modern office developments, there was a safety feature built into the computer system. In the event of a fire, every exit automatically unlocked. The glass door that had sealed us in sprang back and the water poured out into the corridor. We were soaked.

We'd had a bad scare. But it looked like we were going to walk – rather than swim – out of here.

Obviously, we weren't going to take the lifts. With water spraying all around us, we made our way to the emergency stairs and began the long climb down. I was beginning to wonder how we'd get back to Camden Town. It was unlikely that a taxi would stop for us, not when we both looked like we'd just been for a swim in the River Thames.

In fact, I needn't have worried. We'd reached the ground floor, crossed the reception area and walked through the open doors when two fire engines and a police car pulled up. We stood there, dripping, with the blue lights flashing around us. A bunch of firefighters ran past. Then two police officers arrived. One was Chief Inspector Snape. The other, direct from *Jurassic Park*, was his assistant, Detective Sergeant Boyle.

"Well, well, well," Snape said. "This is a nice surprise." He looked from me to Tim and back again. "Tim Diamond, Nick Diamond – you're under arrest!"

Under Arrest

Chief Inspector Snape and his assistant, Detective Sergeant Boyle, were the last two people I wanted to meet ... and that's at the end of a long list. They'd arrested me twice when I was chasing after Johnny Naples and a fortune in diamonds – and they'd actually thrown me in jail to help them find a master criminal known as the Fence, even though I hadn't done anything wrong.

Snape was pink and chunky. Imagine a professional wrestler getting out of a very hot bath and you'll get the general idea. He had narrow and suspicious eyes, which is to say that the left one was narrow and the right one was suspicious: it's just a shame they didn't match. Boyle had the sort of black curly hair that you'd normally find in someone's armpit but, unfortunately, it was on his head. At some stage in his life, he'd broken his nose and it had only improved his face. When Boyle smiled, I'd actually seen little kids cry. He was wearing a bomber jacket and faded jeans. If they faded any more, they'd disappear, and all I can say is that I wished Boyle would go with them.

The two of them had known Tim long before he became a private detective. After my brother left university, he'd joined the police force and Snape had been his senior officer. It hadn't been a happy experience for either of them. Tim had arrested an old lady and helped an armed robber across the road. He'd given speeding tickets to three parked cars, a steamroller and a hearse driving into a cemetery. And he'd managed to handcuff himself to a moving bus. All of this had occurred in his first week, by which time the crime figures in London had already reached an all-time high. By the end of the year, criminals were sending him Christmas cards. Snape wasn't amused.

The moment we came out of Battersea Tower, Boyle grabbed hold of us and threw us in the back of a police van. It was just a shame that he'd forgotten to open the doors. He picked us up off the road and threw us in a second time, and a few minutes later we set off. I think the driver must have chosen the way with the most twists and turns, the most bumps and potholes, because we were thrown around like two odd socks in a washing machine. By the time we arrived at Battersea Police Station, the two of us were well and truly battered.

A scowling police officer led us down to an interrogation room. "Any chance of a cup of tea?" Tim asked.

"Yes," the officer replied. "I'm going to have one right now."

We didn't get anything, of course. Not even a glass of water. The interrogation room was a square box with a table, four chairs and a barred window with no view. We sat down. We were still soaking wet and our clothes dripped onto the cement floor around us. After about ten minutes, the door opened and Snape and Boyle came in, glancing at us as if they were surprised to find us there. We were surrounded by puddles and they hadn't bothered to bring a towel. They sat down opposite us.

"So," Snape began, "what have you got to say for yourselves?"

"I want to see a lawyer," Tim said.

"You'll be seeing an emergency doctor specializing in fractures and soft-tissue injuries unless you give us some answers fast," Snape replied. He turned to me. "How do you fancy half an hour on your own with my friend, Boyle?"

"If he was with me, I wouldn't be on my own," I pointed out.

Snape's face darkened. "Don't try to be clever with me, Diamond. I've got you for breaking and entering, criminal trespass and vandalism. What were you doing at Battersea Tower?"

"We were invited there for a meeting. That's not against the law. We did nothing wrong," I said. "We walked in and the doors closed behind us. We were trying to get out. And we didn't break anything."

"That's right!" Tim said. "The lift tried to kill us. And the sprinkler system!"

"It was an ambush," I explained. "Somebody wanted us dead. They must have hacked into the office computer. They used all the security systems in the building to trap us and then they tried to drown us."

"Do you really expect me to believe that?" Snape growled.

"Why not? It's the truth."

"I'll get the truth." Boyle had taken out a wooden cosh. He waved it at us menacingly, then whacked it three times against the palm of his hand. There was a brief silence. Boyle whimpered.

"Are you all right, Boyle?" Snape asked.

"No, sir. I think I've broken my hand."

"I have warned you about that..." He turned back to us. "Now look what you've done!"

"We haven't done anything," I insisted.

I glanced at Boyle, who was examining his hand,

trying to make the fingers work. Snape was sitting beside him, chewing invisible gum. I wondered if I should tell them about Waverly, MI6 and zEbra but decided against it. Snape hadn't believed the bits of our story that were actually believable. So what would he make of the rest of it?

I wasn't going to find out. At that moment, the door opened and a third police officer came in. This time it was a woman, dressed in a navy-blue uniform with the chequerboard tie and matching hat of the Metropolitan Police. She had silver embroidery on her shoulders and around her neck, and a row of medals across her chest. She was about fifty with grey hair, grey eyes and grey lips. Snape and Boyle sprang to attention when she came in, and that was when I realized she was only about five feet tall. The two of them towered over her but they still seemed nervous. She was clearly the one in charge.

"Good evening, ma'am!" Snape exclaimed. "This is a surprise!"

"No need to get up, Snape," the new arrival snapped. She spoke in the same way that a dog barks but without the bright eyes or the wagging tail. She'd only been in the room for a few seconds and already I was afraid she was going to bite. "What's happening here?" she demanded.

"We have two suspects we're questioning about an office break-in," Snape explained.

"But it's the middle of the night!"

In fact, it must have been about half past nine. I glanced at my watch but after the soaking it had received, I had a feeling it might not be accurate. The two hands had come loose and were floating under the glass. "Who are you?" I asked.

The woman scowled as if she was surprised I needed to ask. "I'm Assistant Chief Commissioner Davina Dawson," she said. "And who are you?"

"I'm Nick Diamond," I said. "And this is my big brother, Tim."

"How do you do?" Tim stood up and held out a hand. Water poured out of his sleeve.

"So, you're the Diamond brothers!" Dawson smiled for the first time.

I wasn't sure what surprised me more: that she'd heard of us or that she wasn't reaching for the pepper spray! "I know all about you," she went on. "The brilliant investigator and his older brother."

"Actually, Nick is younger than me," Tim said.

"Oh, I was referring to Nick!" She beamed at me. "What a pleasure to meet you. I've heard lots of great things about you. The case of the Falcon's Malteser and that business with Johnny Powers! I'm very much hoping you'll join the police when you finish your GCSEs."

"Police? No thanks!"

"I'm sorry to hear that. So, what do you want to be when you grow up?"

"Alive." It was true. In the last year I'd lost count of the number of people who'd tried to make sure it didn't happen.

"Excuse me, ma'am..." Snape looked completely lost. "I think there must be some mistake. These two broke into Battersea Tower. They set off the fire alarms and they've done thousands of pounds' worth of damage."

"There certainly *has* been a mistake!" Dawson replied.

"Treating these young men like criminals and bringing them down here. I want them released at once. In fact, I'm going to see to it myself." As if to illustrate her words, she threw open the door.

"With respect, ma'am, we've only just begun our questioning," Snape muttered. Next to him, Boyle was cradling his fingers, which had swelled up like sausages.

"And what questions do you have, Chief Inspector?"

"Well..."

"I might suggest one. What's the speed limit in Kensington Road?"

"I'm sorry, ma'am?"

"It's something you might need to know when you're transferred to the traffic unit! Do I make myself clear?"

She swept out of the room. Tim followed. Before I went, I turned to Boyle and held out a hand. "No hard feelings," I said.

Without thinking, he let me take his hand and I gave it a good squeeze. He was still screaming when we reached the staircase.

"I'm sorry about that misunderstanding," Dawson

said as we climbed up to the ground floor. She really was very small. She had to heave herself up every step, her medals clinking together as she went. "The sooner the two of you are out of here, the better," she added.

"Any chance of a taxi?" Tim asked.

"No. I'm afraid we don't have the budget. But you can take a tube. There's a station just round the corner. Go past the hospital and it's opposite the funeral parlour, next to the cemetery. You can't miss it."

Was I imagining things or was there something a bit gloomy about what she had said ... a hospital, a funeral parlour and a cemetery all in one sentence? But right then, I didn't care. The important thing was that we were being released. For some reason, one of the most senior police officers in the country had decided to help us, and there was nothing that Snape or Boyle could do about it. We were free!

We climbed the last steps and went into a reception area with a couple of burly policemen sitting on plastic chairs. They had obviously been waiting for us and got up the moment we appeared. There was a double door in front of us with frosted-glass windows. I could just make out the glow of the street lights on the other side.

The way out.

"I do apologize for what happened," Dawson said. "But I can assure you that the police will be pressing no charges. You're free to leave!"

She gestured at the door and at the same time I became aware of a sound coming from the other side, a soft growling like a dozen hungry animals. It was a sound I recognized. The last time I'd heard it, I'd been in the multistorey car park in...

Motorbikes. That was what was waiting for us in the street.

One of the policemen opened the doors and at once I saw them – a long line of motorbikers opposite the police station. Tommy and Troy were in the middle. As for the others, they could have been mirror reflections of each other with their beards, dark glasses, round helmets and Union Jacks. In fact, I wish they had been mirror reflections because that would have meant there were half as many of them. As it was, I counted five on each side of the two leaders, making a dirty dozen in total.

We were safe so long as we stayed in the police station. The moment we stepped outside, we would be minced. But the Assistant Chief Commissioner didn't seem to be aware of any danger.

"Goodnight," she trilled. "I do hope we'll meet again one day."

I turned round. "Actually, I think I may have left my Oyster card downstairs."

"We'll send it to you."

"But I need it for the tube."

"I can lend you the fare."

It was amazing. We were trapped. Some of the most unpleasant men in the history of motorcycling were waiting to kill us, but as far as she was concerned,

everything was just fine. Tim took a step forward and I grabbed his sleeve. Water trickled through my fingers.

"Tim," I whispered. "We need to go back inside."

"Why?"

"We can't leave! It's not safe." I nudged him hard and, at that moment, the line of motorbikers revved their engines, as if they were getting tired of waiting, and now even Tim was aware of them. His face went a cheesy white and he turned to Dawson. "Do you have a toilet?" he squeaked.

"I'm sorry?" Dawson scowled.

"I need to use a toilet." Tim pushed me towards the door. "You go ahead, Nick. I'll catch up with you later."

"Thanks, Tim!" That was typical of him.

"The toilet's closed," one of the policemen growled. They were standing very close to us now. It was almost as if they were preparing to push us out into the street.

"What exactly is the matter?" Dawson asked.

"Those people outside want to kill us!" I explained.

"Nonsense! They're just a group of motorbike enthusiasts enjoying the evening air. What makes you think they're interested in you?"

"They've already tried to kill us twice!"

"You have a wonderful imagination, Nick." She put an arm around me, her medals tinkling with pleasure. "But I'm afraid it's time for you to go."

I couldn't let her do this. I had to find a way to make her let me stay.

"I'm a shoplifter!" I shouted.

"I'm sorry?"

"You were quite wrong about me ... what you said downstairs. I'm not a nice boy at all. I steal from lots of different shops. I'm like Robin Hood, only worse. I steal from the poor and give to the rich."

I was lying of course. I'd managed to come up with the one sure way to get myself locked up, safely, in the police station. I had to persuade them that I was a criminal and make them arrest me again. "Last week I stole a car!" I went on. "And I broke the speed limit. I drove up the M1 at ninety miles an hour!"

"And he didn't fasten his seat belt!" Tim chimed in. By some miracle, he'd realized what I was trying to do.

"I hate seat belts. And I drove on the right side of the road."

"You mean the wrong side of the road," Tim said.

"Exactly. The right side of the road."

"Talking on your mobile phone."

"I wasn't just talking. I was watching YouTube!"

Dawson waved a finger. "You're just joking with us," she said. "I don't believe a word of it."

"Then you're an idiot!" I shouted. "There you are! I've insulted a police officer. You've got to lock us up again. My brother, Tim, wants to kill the Archbishop of London."

"He hasn't got a prayer!" Tim agreed.

"You have to put us in a cell!"

But Dawson had had enough. "I have work to do," she said. "It's time for our guests to leave."

And right then I saw something in her face that had been there all the time but which I hadn't seen before. She was still smiling – in fact, if her lips stretched any wider, they'd disappear behind her head. And there was a strange gleam in her eyes.

She knew what she was doing! She hadn't been surprised by the appearance of a dozen motorbikes outside the police station. She'd been expecting them!

And then I remembered the question that Dawson had just asked Snape when we were in the interrogation room. *What's the speed limit in Kensington Road?* It had struck me as odd at the time. Why, of all the streets in London, had she chosen that one? I had thought it was just a coincidence. How could she possibly have known that Tim and I had almost been killed in that exact street that very same day? But now I realized that, as impossible as it seemed, she was part of it too. Mr Waverly had warned us when we were at MI6. He had said that the White Crusaders had a lot of powerful people behind them. Assistant Chief Commissioner Davina Dawson was one of them. There could be no other explanation.

"Goodnight!" she said.

The two policemen grabbed hold of us and propelled us through the door, immediately slamming it shut behind us. I heard the locks being turned. And suddenly, we were alone with our backs to the police station and a vicious motorbike gang waiting in front of us.

"What are we going to do?" Tim wailed. "They want to kill us!"

I'd become aware of a rumbling sound and, looking up the street, I saw a rubbish truck making its way towards us. In a few seconds it would pass right in front of us.

"Rubbish," I muttered.

"No, Nick. They really do."

"Follow me, Tim..."

I ran forward and threw myself onto the rubbish truck just as it reached us, grabbing hold of the handles at the side. Tim did the same. The two of us clung on to the steel wall with the stench of rotting waste all around us and the huge wheels crunching down on the road as the truck continued round the corner. To the bikers it must have looked like a magic trick. One moment we were there, the next we had disappeared. And the best news was that it took them several moments more to work out what had actually happened.

I saw a row of plastic dustbins ahead and felt the truck slow down as it prepared to stop.

"Now!" I shouted.

Tim and I let go, hitting the edge of the pavement and immediately breaking into a run. Behind us, I heard the sound of the motorbike engines rising up in a howl of anger that filled the night sky. We came to the cemetery that Dawson had mentioned. It was tiny, left over from the nineteenth century, and, fortunately, it had a low fence. The two of us jumped over and we continued through the gravestones. I was just glad that we wouldn't be needing two of them ... not tonight anyway.

Dawson had also told us that we would find a tube station nearby and, sure enough, it was there. We jumped over the barrier and ran down the escalator. It took Tim a little longer than it had taken me – but then, he had chosen the up escalator. There was a tube train waiting at the platform and we flung ourselves into it, taking two seats as the doors closed.

I managed to catch my breath. "We're going to Scotland," I said.

"Are you sure?" Tim asked. "It said Edgware via King's Cross on the front of the train."

"London isn't safe any more, Tim. We've got to go to Hare Island with MI6 and their bunch of commandos. It's the only way out of this mess."

Even as I spoke the words, I regretted them. I've got nothing against Scotland but right then it was the last place I wanted to go. And it was almost as if the tube train agreed. I heard the scream of the wheels as it carried us forward, plunging us into the tunnel. Light turned to darkness. The story of my life.

Rough Crossing

On a bright sunny day, the fishing village of Gargle might have been worth visiting, but with thick clouds, the rain slicing down and a steel-coloured sea chopping at the harbour walls, it was about as miserable a place as it was possible to be. It was as if summer had forgotten to come here. The shops were closed. The streets were filled with puddles. The fishermen were looking as cheerful as the fish they had just caught and the seagulls weren't even bothering to fly. They were sitting in the middle of the road like they were hoping to be run over by a bus.

It was four o'clock in the afternoon. Tim and I had taken the coach up from London to Aberdeen and then come across by taxi. The driver had been surprised when we'd asked to be taken to Gargle.

"Nobody ever goes there," he had explained in a Scottish accent so thick you could have wrapped yourself in it to stay warm. "It's a grim wee place. Have you ever been to Grimsby?"

"No," Tim said.

"Well, it's grimmer. Have you been to Dulwich?"

"No."

"Well, it's duller. Have you been to Crapstone—?"

"Just keep your eyes on the road," I cut in.

The village only had one hotel and the hotel only had one star. The Gargler's Arms was a two-storey building that bulged in the middle as if it had been squeezed at both ends. The roof was sagging and there was a trickle of grey smoke leaking out of the chimney. There was no welcoming fire, incidentally; it was just the head waiter having a cigarette in the fireplace. The flagstones were cold and grey. So was the receptionist.

After she'd signed us in, she handed us a key and grunted, "Room three."

"And where is that?" Tim asked.

"It's next to room two. Breakfast is at seven. Do you like porridge?"

"No," Tim said.

"Then you won't be having breakfast." She crossed out both our names on the guest list. "Do you want a morning piper?"

"Don't you mean paper?"

"No. The owner plays the bagpipes every morning at six."

"Does he live in the hotel?"

"He's in room four."

"When's checkout?" Tim asked.

The receptionist thought for a moment. "Usually, it's about ten minutes after people check in," she said sourly.

We left her and went into the bar, where two men and a woman were sitting at a table in the corner with a bottle of whisky and three glasses. We already knew

Flint. He was the driver who had saved us at the car park in Kensington. Just from looking at him, I could tell he was dangerous. He probably knew twenty-six ways to kill a human being using his bare hands and another two ways using his teeth. He was the one in charge.

"Let me introduce you," he said.

"It's all right," Tim said. "Nick and I already know each other."

Flint had been chewing gum and, for a moment, I thought he was going to swallow it. "I want to introduce you to the team," he explained. "This is Blake and this is Marcie."

"Which is which?" Tim asked.

It should have been easy to tell. Blake was in his forties, built like a street fighter but not the sort of street you'd want to live in. He had dark, thoughtful eyes but I was pretty sure the thoughts were all about death and maiming. Marcie had a hungry, pale face, a square chin, a permanent scowl and colourless hair cut by a barber who hadn't known when to stop ... or

even where to start. She was sitting with her elbows on the table. She had short arms and big fists.

All three of them had dressed for action with camouflage jackets, khaki trousers, balaclavas and combat boots. Not for the first time, I wondered if Tim's choice of Harry Potter T-shirt, pink cardigan and bobble hat had been a good idea. You could say he was dressed to kill – but only if the enemy died laughing.

"All right," Flint began. "We'll be leaving as soon as it's dark."

"Can't we wait until it stops raining?" Tim asked.

"No!" Flint shook his head. "The bad weather is on our side. It means there's less chance of our being seen." He threw back his whisky and poured himself another glass.

"Do you know how to control a canoe?" Flint asked.

"I've only ever seen one in a zoo," Tim replied. "I suppose you have to feed it grass or straw..."

"Not a gnu. A canoe. We'll be making the crossing in three folding canoes."

"Wait a minute." Tim leaned forward. "If they fold, won't they sink?"

"We fold them after we come out of the water. It makes them easier to carry and smaller to hide."

"Why don't we just take a ferry?"

"Because there's only one ferry a week to Hare Island and everyone on board has to carry ID." Flint glared at us. "You can't have forgotten what Mr Waverly told you..."

"Who was Mr Waverly again?" Tim asked.

Flint took a deep breath. "Hare Island is like a

miniature country," he reminded us. "It has its own laws and its own armed police force working alongside the White Crusaders. And it's totally British. It's the only place in the world you can get arrested for singing the national anthem out of tune. Neville Fairfax rules over it like a medieval king, sitting in his castle up at Seagull's Rise. If we're going to have any hope of surviving, we're going to have to move quickly."

"I agree," Tim said. "If we run, we might just be able to catch the coach back to London..."

"No. We have to move quickly once we're on the island. We're going to be in and out in one day. The helicopter will be waiting for us at exactly four o'clock tomorrow afternoon. This is the plan. We cross over to the island in canoes, break into Seagull's Rise, release zEbra, break out again and reach the rendezvous point, trying not to be taken prisoner, tortured or shot."

"Does anyone have a plan that *doesn't* involve being taken prisoner, tortured or shot?" Tim asked.

"No. This is the only plan we've got."

There was silence around the table. Tim wiped his nose with a hankie and slipped it into his pocket.

"All right," I went on. "You've told us your plan, but what you haven't said is how Tim and I fit into it all. Mr Waverly told us we had special skills. In fact, he said we were exactly what he needed. What did he mean by that?"

"OK," Flint replied. "This is how it works. Neville Fairfax lives in Seagull's Rise and he's surrounded by armed guards. His head of security is a man called Milton Grove."

"That sounds like his address," I said.

"I wouldn't make jokes about him, kid. He's vicious. Twenty years in the prison service. As a prisoner. They only let him out because they were too scared to keep him in. He started with knife crime – he stole a knife. After that it was attempted murder and then, on the third attempt, actual murder. Now he works for Fairfax. He's devoted to him."

"So where do we come in?" I asked.

Flint nodded. "As well as guards, Fairfax employs

a lot of servants at Seagull's Rise," he said. "There are butlers and housekeepers and lady's maids, cooks and footmen ... all looking after him and his rich friends. Recently, he advertised for a boot boy."

"What does the boot boy do?" I asked. I wasn't liking the sound of this.

"He polishes the boots. He also cleans the toilets, sweeps the floors and takes out the rubbish. He starts at six in the morning and works until midnight. He's treated like a dog."

"They rub his tummy and take him for walks?" Tim asked.

"No. It's a horrible job. The previous boot boy only lasted three days."

"What happened to him?"

"He got the boot. Nick is going to take his place."

"Am I?" This was news to me.

"We've already applied on your behalf," Blake cut in. "You've got an interview tomorrow at ten o'clock."

"What happens if he doesn't get the job?" Tim asked.

"It doesn't make any difference," Flint replied. "The point is that the two of you have been cleared to travel up to the castle in the cable car. I'm sure Mr Waverly told you, it's the only way in."

"And out," I added.

"Exactly. This is what happens. You take the cable car at nine o'clock. Your brother will travel with you."

"Am I applying for a job?" Tim asked.

"No. Nick can't go in alone because he's a minor. And if you tell me he's never worked in a mine, I'll kill you. He's under sixteen. So you're going in as Nick's big brother ... you're looking after him."

"That makes a change," I said.

"Now, this is the most important thing. The cable car can only be activated from the castle. Fairfax wants to be absolutely sure he knows who is coming in and out of the castle. After the interview, you go straight back to the cable car station."

"How will we know where to find it?" Tim said.

Flint gritted his teeth. "You'll have seen it when you got out of the cable car. The station is a big room full of machinery and most of the time there's nobody there. The system is fully automated. All you have to do is find the green button on the console and press it. That will send the cable car back to the bottom of the mountain and allow Blake, Marcie and me to climb in. It's a three-minute journey each way."

"So you'll be with us in nine minutes!" Tim exclaimed.

"No. Three plus three is six. We'll be with you in six minutes."

"Unless you stop to take photographs of the view."

"We won't. When we get to the top, we'll find zEbra and get him out of there. We'll blow up all of Neville Fairfax's computers to stop him using them again and then we'll take the cable car down, get to the helicopter and go home. Do you have any questions?"

I had plenty of questions. Like: what was I doing here, who had thought up this crazy plan and how could I get out of all this without being shot? But from the way Flint was sitting there, chewing his gum and watching me with those pitiless eyes,

I knew there was no point in asking them.

"All right," he said. "You need to get some rest. I'll have supper sent up to your room. Would you like some boiled haggis with tatties and neeps?"

"I'd prefer something edible," Tim said.

"Well, you'll need something hot inside you when you get into those canoes." He slid the bottle towards Tim. "We'll wake you up at midnight."

I made sure we left the whisky behind. Tim wasn't good with alcohol. I'd seen him pass out after eating a bowl of sherry trifle. We climbed up a rickety staircase to a small room with twin beds and a view of the harbour. The rain was still pelting down. Water streamed down the windows and dripped through a hole in the roof. The sea looked like it was trying to tear itself apart.

Flint had left clothes for us to wear during the crossing: thickly knitted jerseys and waterproof trousers, jackets and army boots – all of them black. There was also a jar of dark-blue face paint in a plastic tub.

"What's this for?" Tim asked.

"It's camouflage," I said. "You put it on your face so you can't be seen."

Tim smeared himself with the stuff, then looked in the mirror. "I can still see myself," he said.

I didn't bother to explain. Half an hour later, the receptionist brought up our supper: two bowls of Scotch broth, two Scotch eggs and a butterscotch tart. We ate quickly, then stretched ourselves out on the beds. The springs squeaked and groaned – or maybe that was Tim.

It was only half past six but I was already tired. It had been a long day. I lay back with my head on the pillow and ten minutes later I was having my first nightmares about kidnapped computer experts and cable cars, motorbikers with machine guns, canoes folding themselves up as I tried to paddle across a cold, choppy sea. The worst of it was, I wasn't actually asleep. How had I got into this mess? Just a few days ago I'd been looking forward to the summer holidays. Now I was wondering if I'd even survive them.

The next thing I knew there was a knock at the door

and I woke up to hear the wind howling outside and to see Flint looking in, his face covered with the dark-blue camouflage, his eyes gleaming with excitement. I could tell he was the sort of person who would look forward to paddling across a freezing cold sea in a force-nine gale with almost certain death on the other side. He, Blake and Marcie had actually chosen this style of life. Personally, I hadn't even bothered with the Scouts.

But I had no choice. I wasn't aware that I had managed to doze off, but now I dragged myself off the bed and shook Tim awake.

"Not today, thanks," he muttered. His eyes were still closed.

I reached for a glass of water and poured it over him.

Ten minutes later, we were dressed in our water-proofs and army boots. We'd camouflaged our faces. I'd persuaded Tim to leave his bobble hat behind. We made our way downstairs and joined the others in the reception area. Flint, Marcie and Blake were sorting out their weapons. I'd never seen so many guns, knives and hand grenades being loaded into their different pockets. If any of them fell out of their canoe, they'd sink like a stone. Tim and I weren't being armed, of course. Perhaps that was sensible. Hand Tim a gun and he'd only succeed in blowing off his own head – or, worse still, mine. Even so, I felt strangely naked as we headed out into the night air, like an oven-ready chicken destined for the deep freeze.

The rain was horizontal now, whipped sideways by the wind. The sea was even rougher than it had been earlier, hurling itself onto the quay and desperately trying to cling on to the surface before being dragged back again. There was no moon. A single lamp post glimmered with a lamp that barely managed to illuminate the post. Fat puddles spread out beneath our feet. My fingers were already numb. So this was what summer was like in Scotland! Three canoes were waiting for us, lying on the quay like wounded animals. The paddles were beside them. There was no sign of an outboard motor.

"I'll go first," Flint shouted. "Then you and your brother. Then Blake and Marcie behind. If we get separated, keep heading east." He handed me a compass. "Have you ever used one of these?"

"No," I said. "I've never seen the point."

"Just keep the arrow on E. Are you ready?" He didn't wait for me to reply. "Then let's go."

We dragged the canoes over to the side of the quay and lowered them into the sea, which leapt up as if to devour them. I was already soaked and we hadn't even begun the crossing. Flint jumped into his canoe first, then Blake and Marcie did the same. I managed to climb into our canoe, even though it was rocking crazily beneath me. Finally, Tim followed.

I looked over my shoulder. Tim had his back to me so we were facing in opposite directions. "I think something's gone wrong," I said.

"What do you mean?"

"We've got to look the same way, Tim. I'm going forwards. You're going backwards. If we both start paddling, we're not going to move!"

"You might be right."

Tim climbed out again. Then he got in the right

way. Flint had already set off. Blake and Marcie were waiting for us, battling with their paddles to keep their canoe steady, almost invisible behind the rain.

"Are you ready?" I shouted.

"No!" Tim shouted back.

It didn't matter. We set off anyway, digging into the surface of the water with the paddles and driving ourselves forwards. With just half a dozen strokes we had left the quay behind us and when I looked back over my shoulder, Gargle was just a vague yellow glow in the distance. Tim was hunched up behind me, although with the blue camouflage paint I could barely see him. Even so, I could make out the water streaming down his face and I was glad that so far he hadn't dropped his paddle.

As we moved forward, the waves seemed to grow in size, rising up around us like grey monsters, lurching at the canoe as we steered our way between them. How far had Mr Waverly said it was to Hare Island? A mile and a half. That wasn't too far, not if you were walking across a park or cycling to school. But we were stuck in the middle of a dark, swirling, raging North Sea with the canoe rising and falling beneath us. It was like being on the world's worst ever fairground ride, knowing that it was too late to get off.

Flint set the pace. I was at the front of our canoe and focused all my attention on the dark muscular figure paddling ahead of us. I could feel the freezing water all around me, punching into my face, trying to scoop me out of the canoe. Tim had vanished. The whole world had gone. It was just me and a million gallons of water. I couldn't breathe. I couldn't cry out. All I could do was pray that somehow it would soon be over. A moment later, it was. I was spluttering, blind, soaking wet ... but we had come out the other side of the wall of water and Flint was there, battling ahead of us, alone in his canoe.

We kept going. The rain lashed into us. The sea crashed onto us. I was lost in a world of water and pain. My fingers were frozen. My arms and shoulders were aching. I was beginning to think it would have been easier to cross the North Sea on the back of a gnu. At least it could have helped by swimming and it might have cheered me up by wagging its tail. How much longer could we keep this up? I had swallowed so much seawater that my stomach was churning and my throat was on fire. And then, just when I was about to give up, I saw a few tiny specks of light ahead of us. It was still the middle of the night and there was no moon, but even so I was aware of a great lump of darkness that might have been a mountain, rising up out of the sea. Could we possibly have reached Hare Island? How long had we been going? It could have been three hours. It could have been three days. Tim muttered something but the wind snatched the words away. And then there was a crunching right underneath me and I realized we had run aground on the shingle. Right in front of us, Flint was standing up, signalling to us to keep quiet. Very vaguely, somewhere in the shadows, I saw trees. The third canoe with Blake and Marcie sliced its way ashore.

We had arrived.

Seagull's Rise

We woke up the next morning, cold and damp, huddled together in an abandoned boathouse. Flint had led us straight to it and although the doors were locked, it had taken him only a few seconds to open them. There were towels and fresh clothes inside. Also, I noticed Flint removing a large silver suitcase

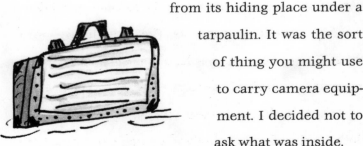 from its hiding place under a tarpaulin. It was the sort of thing you might use to carry camera equipment. I decided not to ask what was inside.

"We've been very lucky," Tim said to me. He pulled off his shoe and poured about half a litre of water onto the ground.

"What do you mean?"

"Well, it's lucky that the boathouse was here and that Mr Flint had a key for the lock and that somebody had left us these dry clothes and towels..."

"I don't think it was luck, Tim," I replied. "I think they've planned it all."

"Really?"

"Yes. They've obviously been thinking about this operation for some time. They've got it all worked out."

Even as I spoke, I was worried. There was a lot that Flint hadn't told us. He obviously knew much more than he was telling – and he hadn't told us very much at all. I wondered how many more surprises would be lying in wait for us throughout the day. That's the trouble with spies. They're not nice people. If you ever see one smiling at you, it's probably because they've just killed you.

As soon as the sun came up, we changed into the new clothes – they fitted perfectly, of course – and wiped the camouflage paint off our faces. Marcie offered us each an energy bar, which she had produced from her backpack, but Tim shook his head, telling her he didn't have enough energy to eat it. Before we left, Flint took out a pair of brand-new blue passports and handed them to Tim and me. "You'll need these," he said. "We've given you false names."

Tim glanced at the front cover. "My name is Passport?" he asked.

"No. The document *is* a passport. Your name is inside."

I opened mine. My face was there sure enough. But the name underneath identified me as Nick Gold.

"I thought that would be easy to remember," Flint said. "Diamonds and Gold."

"This doesn't look anything like me," Tim said.

"You're holding it upside down."

"Oh yes..."

We had new names and new identities. We had jeans and jerseys. We set off back along the beach, heading for the town.

It had been pitch-dark when we'd arrived on Hare Island but as we walked along the shingle, I was able to take in my surroundings. The main town was straight ahead, a collection of ugly grey buildings facing each other across a maze of narrow streets. The only colour came from the Union Jack flags fluttering from the roofs. I think there were more flags than roofs. The streets were almost empty, apart from a few vehicles parked outside the supermarket: two jeeps, a tank and a missile launcher. That told me something about the place where we'd just arrived.

But what really caught my attention was the mountain rising up behind the town. I had vaguely made it out from the canoe but now, in the morning light, I could see it in all its immensity. It was a giant slab of rock and granite perhaps half a mile high with nothing growing on it and no paths leading to the top. The front part was missing. It looked as if the mountain had been sliced in half by a giant knife, leaving a sheer, solid wall that plunged down with no handholds and no footholds. Even the world's most daring goat would have found it impossible to climb.

The castle – Seagull's Rise – was
perched right at the top and on the
very edge, looking down on the town,
which must have looked quite tiny far below. It was a
proper medieval fortress with lots of different towers,
rows of battlements, narrow windows and, of course,
more flags flying at every corner. Three thick wires
looped down from what looked like a wooden platform just under the front wall and I guessed that these
were what supported the cable car. But the car wasn't
running yet. There was no sign of life apart from the
seagulls weaving overhead.

A few early risers began to appear in the high street
as we approached, perhaps on their way to work. Some
of them had shopping bags. All of them had guns.
There was a sense of menace everywhere. Even the
local supermarket had a machine-gun nest outside the
entrance. The cinema was showing an old war film,
Battle of Britain. Spoiler alert: we won. We heard the
growl of a motor and an open-top jeep cruised past with

three black-suited men, scanning the road from behind their dark glasses. This was the official police force. They worked hand in hand with the White Crusaders and I was waiting for them to show up too.

It was crazy. We were only just over a mile from the British coast, but it was as if we'd arrived in a foreign country and the year had somehow gone back to the 1940s and the Second World War. This was Neville Fairfax's private kingdom and everything here was dangerous. If you wanted to live on the island, you had to be as mad as him. If you wanted to die here, you just had to tell him that.

We found a café in the high street and squeezed in around a table. A blonde-haired waitress came over. She looked at us suspiciously and I wondered if she was going to take our order or call the police. "I haven't seen you before," she said.

Flint stared at her. "That's because we haven't been here before," he replied. "What's your name?"

"Heidi." She wasn't smiling and I could feel the tension in the room.

"OK, then, Heidi. We'll have five bacon rolls and five cups of tea. Strong and sweet – like my grandma."

But Heidi didn't move. Next to me, Blake reached into his pocket and I could imagine his hand closing around a gun. She turned to Tim. "Do you have a permit to visit Hare Island?" she demanded.

"Sure." Tim took out his passport. "Here's my ID, Heidi."

She didn't take it. "You're tourists?"

"That's right."

"How long are you staying here?"

"We're here until Friday, Heidi."

She nodded. "All right. Five bacon rolls coming up..."

Heidi disappeared into the kitchen. The moment she had gone, Flint turned to Tim and me. "OK," he whispered. "As soon as you've had some breakfast, get in the cable car. You know what to do."

"Sure," Tim said. "You just told us. We get in the cable car."

"I mean, you know what to do when you get *out of* the cable car."

"We meet Neville Fairfax. And then we send the cable car down for the rest of you," I said.

"Exactly. Just remember. We can't operate the cable car from the lower station. If you don't hit the button, the whole mission is over."

About twenty minutes later, once we'd finished our breakfast, Tim and I headed off. By now there were more people in the streets and quite a few of them glanced in our direction as we walked past. They weren't pleased to see us. There was nothing stranger on Hare Island than a stranger. Very few people visited and I knew I was sticking out like a sore thumb ... which, incidentally, was something I had after all that paddling in the canoe. Two more black-suited policemen passed on the other side of the road. Fortunately, they were deep in conversation and didn't notice us. We kept going, trying not to draw attention to ourselves. It helped that we could see the castle from just about every part of the town. It told us which way to go.

We went up Winston Churchill Street, into Charles Dickens Avenue and across William Shakespeare

Crescent. Everything on Hare Island was named after someone who was both famous and British. The cable car station was on the edge of David Beckham Square. It was a modern brick building, facing the castle like a garage with the front door removed. There were two White Crusaders waiting at the entrance and, for a moment, I wondered what would happen if we ran into Tommy and Troy again. We might have false names but we still had the same faces. Yet we were in luck. These two men had the beards, dark glasses and tattoos like all the other White Crusaders, but it turned out we hadn't met them before.

"What's your business at the castle?" one of them asked while the other examined our passports.

"I'm here to clean boots," I said.

That made them smile. "What about your big brother?" the other one asked.

"He's looking after me."

"All right, Mr Gold. Here's your passport back." The second man held out the passports.

Tim stared at him. "Who's Mr Gold?"

"You are!" I hissed.

The White Crusader was suspicious. "How come he doesn't know his name?" he demanded.

"He's only had it for twenty-eight years," I said. "He's a slow learner."

I snatched the passports and pushed him ahead of me into the cable car station. The cable car itself was a metal box with sliding doors, windows on all sides and two benches facing each other, allowing six people to travel at the same time. We were making the journey alone, though. One of the White Crusaders had taken out a radio transmitter. He spoke briefly, presumably connecting with the control room in the castle. The machinery started up and we found ourselves being lifted, smoothly and silently, rising diagonally through the sky towards Seagull's Rise.

I have to admit, the next three minutes provided us with a fantastic view and if I'd been on holiday, rather than heading for almost certain death, I might have enjoyed it. The town disappeared behind us, dwindling into the distance as we climbed higher and higher. We hovered over green fields with the cut-off mountain in front of us and the sea behind and, suddenly, we could see from one end of the island to the other ... a distance of no more than a mile. There was only one main road on Hare Island and I could see it twisting from west to east like a grey ribbon. At four o'clock, a helicopter would be landing to collect us. I just hoped it knew which end to land on.

We were about halfway up now, passing right across the centre of a lake filled with emerald-green water. The sun was reflecting off the surface. It was the middle of summer but it still looked freezing cold. There were some farm buildings on the other side and I could see a few sheep grazing on the long grass: British sheep, of course. Their coats had been dyed red, white and blue. The castle was looming up ahead of us and the closer we got, the more sinister it seemed – a great stone beast crouching on the edge of the mountain as if about to leap. Now we could see the control room, open to the elements and built underneath the front wall, with a giant metal cylinder slowly turning, reeling us in. A shadow fell over us as we were pulled through the entrance. We could hear the grinding of machinery. The cable car slid onto two tracks and came to a halt. We were in.

The door slid open and at the same time a man, dressed in black, with a black cap, black gloves and black boots, marched over to us. "Mr Gold?" he asked.

"That's me!" Tim exclaimed. He'd repeated his false name fifty times during the journey and, finally, he'd got used to it.

"It's me too," I said.

The man turned to me. "Ah yes! Nick Gold! My name is Milton Grove. I'm the head of security at Seagull's Rise. Would you like to follow me?"

"That depends on where you're going," Tim said.

"I'm taking you to see Mr Fairfax. For the interview."

So, this was the famous Milton Grove that Flint had told us about. He was meant to be the world's most dangerous ex-prisoner but he didn't look that dangerous to me. He was small and neat with round glasses and thinning hair. It would have been easy to mistake him for a primary school teacher – if you ignored the uniform and the gun in a holster across his chest. I noticed that he had prison tattoos on his neck and on the fingers of both hands: "VOLE and HATE."

"Shouldn't that be love and hate?" I asked him.

"No," he said. "I hate voles."

The three of us set off, but before we left, I took a quick look around the control room, checking it out for when we came back later. There was a desk covered in old-fashioned equipment, TV monitors and metal boxes with knobs and wires. And there, right in the middle, was a block of wood with a large green button that would send the cable car back to the bottom of the mountain and then straight up again ... this time with Flint, Marcie and Blake inside. An overweight mechanic dressed in brown overalls was sitting in a chair, drinking coffee, but apart from him there was nobody else in the room. Somehow we had to find our way back here. We'd hit the mechanic if he was still here. Then we'd hit the button. Until then, we were on our own.

We followed Grove over to a pair of metal doors, which slid open to reveal an industrial lift on the other side. That made sense. Supplies would have to be brought up from the town and then carried into the castle – and this was the easiest way. Grove pressed a button and we were carried, very slowly, up to the next floor. When the doors opened again, we found ourselves inside the actual castle, with an arched corridor stretching into the distance. There were oil paintings of British kings and queens hanging on the brickwork and I recognized a few of them. Henry the Eighth was the fat one with the beard. Queen Victoria was dressed in black, with her hands folded as if she had stomach ache. Charles the First was the one missing his head. We turned off and passed a series of heavy wooden doors, tables with candlesticks, old chests ... that sort of stuff. The whole place was silent, but with walls a metre thick, someone could be screaming on the other side and we wouldn't know.

We went up a staircase, round a corner and down another passageway with a single door at the far end. Grove knocked. He didn't wait for an answer, or perhaps we couldn't hear it. He opened the door and we went in.

Neville Fairfax was sitting, tapping at a computer on the other side of a solid antique desk in what was obviously his study. There was a stone fireplace blazing on one side, floor-to-ceiling bookshelves and two windows looking out over a courtyard that had four walls, one of them studded with bullet holes. Something growled and I saw a dog – a British bulldog – sitting on a rug in front of the fireplace. I didn't like the way it was looking at us, the flames reflecting in its nasty little eyes. Its mouth was open and it was drooling, great globs of saliva cascading over its extremely sharp teeth like a very small, slow-motion waterfall.

Fairfax looked up as we came in. He examined me with eyes that weren't any nicer than the dog's. "Do you like animals?" he asked.

"We've only just met Mr Grove but he seems nice enough," I replied.

Fairfax half smiled. "I was talking about Brit. My dog." Hearing its name, the dog whined and wagged the little

stump that was all it had for a tail. "He's a superb guard dog, which is just as well as he's bitten most of the guards. He used to be looked after by a kitchen hand but Brit bit him too."

"Was that the hand that fed him?"

Fairfax nodded. "I can see you and I are going to get along. Sit down!"

There were two seats opposite him. Tim and I sat next to each other. Grove stayed by the door.

Quickly, I recalled what Mr Waverly had told us about Neville Fairfax. This was the man who wanted to make Britain great again and planned to start another world war just so he could kill lots of foreigners. First of all, he was going to take over the UK. He had kidnapped a genius computer hacker – zEbra – and he was going to force him to break into the government's computers. Once he'd done that, there would be no stopping him. He would be in charge of the army, the navy, the air force, the police. With a single touch of the button, he could do almost anything.

That was the plan. But what about the man?

Everything about Neville Fairfax spelled paranoia ... not, in fact, the easiest word to spell. First of all, there were those black, deathly eyes. He had grey lips and uneven teeth. His hair, what was left of it, was grey too and I noticed flakes of dandruff on the slopes of his shoulders. His fingers, folded in front of him, seemed a little too long for his hands. Overall, he was thin to the point of scrawny. In fact, I'd seen skeletons in better shape. He was wearing an old-fashioned three-piece suit with a Union Jack tie and a handkerchief poking out of his top pocket, but the clothes didn't look right on him; he seemed to be hiding in them.

"So, you're Nick Gold," he said.

"That's right. And this is Tim Gold. He's my brother."

"Nice to meet you, Mr Cartax," Tim said.

Fairfax ignored him. He was examining me with interest and there was something about the way those dark eyes settled on me that made me shudder. "So you think you'd make a good boot boy?" he asked.

"I'd say I'm a shoe-in," I replied.

"How do you feel about cleaning toilets?"

"I've got nothing to loos."

"What is the full name of Her Majesty the Queen?"

This was a trick question. There was a sudden silence in the room and I knew that if I got this wrong, I'd be out. But I was lucky. "Elizabeth Alexandra Mary Windsor," I replied. I'd seen the answer tattooed on Grove's neck.

Fairfax nodded. "Congratulations!" he exclaimed – but without much enthusiasm. "You've got the job. Grove will take you to your room. You'll meet the other staff tonight and you'll be told exactly what the job entails."

Was it really as easy as that? Something was wrong. It had to be. This was meant to be an interview but he'd only asked me three questions.

I got up to leave but just then Tim cut in. "Wait a minute, Mr Earwax. We haven't talked about salary..."

I rolled my eyes. Tim had barely spoken up until now, but why had he decided to ask about money? Money didn't matter. I planned to be out of this place in about an hour and a half – long before the first pay packet arrived.

Fairfax sneered at him. "It's four pounds an hour. Plus, he gets three meals a day."

"Suppose we were to make it three pounds an hour and four meals a day?"

Fairfax shrugged. "Very well, Mr Gold."

"What about holidays?" Tim went on. "I absolutely insist he gets two weeks a year – and no argument!"

"All right. Whatever you say. But everyone else gets a month." Fairfax stood up. He was much shorter than I'd imagined. "I think that concludes our discussion. Grove will show you to your room..."

Fairfax gestured and Grove led us out into the corridor. We followed him through a twisting stone labyrinth of corridors and doorways, passing a few other staff members on the way. There was a house-maid carrying a bundle of linen, a butler carrying a silver tray and glasses, and two more security men in black uniforms carrying machine guns. These last two reminded me that this place was dangerous. Fairfax made the rules and there were no rules against filling Tim and me with bullet holes. We took one flight of stairs up, two more down, continued along yet another passageway – this one lined with suits of armour – and stopped at another door.

"This will be your room," Grove said. He opened the door.

It wasn't exactly a luxury suite. The room was part of the castle dungeons, a converted cell – and Fairfax hadn't wasted any money on the conversion. The walls were bare, the window barred. The bed was a plank of wood and when they'd finished making the bed, they'd used the wood shavings to fill the mattress. There was a sink with a single cold tap and a wardrobe with a pair of blue shorts, a white shirt and a red waistcoat on a hanger. It was my boot-boy uniform and, frankly, I wouldn't have been seen dead in it, although it occurred to me that if things went wrong in the next hour, I might be.

"You need to get changed," Grove said. He pointed at the cupboard. "I'll come back for you in an hour. Wait for me. I don't want you wandering around Seagull's Rise on your own."

He left, closing the door behind him.

I listened until his footsteps had faded away into the distance. An hour! That was plenty of time to find our way back to the cable car station – always assuming we could find it. Suddenly, I wanted to get out. I had a bad feeling about all this. The sooner Flint and the others arrived, the better.

"Are you ready?" I asked.

Tim was examining the window. He tugged at the bars. "I don't think we can bend these," he said.

"We don't need to, Tim. He didn't lock the door."

"Oh." He went over to the door and opened it.

But it wasn't going to be that simple.

There was a soft growling from out in the corridor. Grove had told us he wanted us to stay in the cell until he got back and he'd left some insurance behind. Brit, the brutal British bulldog, was sitting in the corridor. Seeing us, it stood up and glared with its ugly eyes, drawing back its mouth to show off its vicious teeth.

"Do you think it wants walkies?" Tim asked.

"I don't think so, Tim." I closed the door again.

We weren't going anywhere.

The Green Button

"All right," I said. "We've got to work this out. We're stuck in a cell in a castle filled with crazy people. We have to get back to the cable car station and hit the green button. But there's a savage dog outside the door that'll tear us to pieces before we can take a step. So what do we do?"

Tim thought for a moment. Then his eyes lit up. "I've got an idea!" He took a bag of jelly babies out of his pocket.

"Where did you get those?" I asked.

"I bought them for the coach."

"And how exactly are they going to help us?"

"We can give one to Brute, the brittle, bullish big dog."

"You mean ... Brit, the brutal British bulldog?"

"That's what I said. Burt, the bitter Scottish hotdog. The one outside the door!"

"And what then?"

"While it's eating the jelly baby, we'll run away."

I have to say, it was one of the worst ideas I'd ever heard, but right then I couldn't think of anything else. Maybe the jelly baby would distract the dog long enough for us to slip out the door. So I kept my mouth shut as Tim fished inside the packet.

"What colour do you think it'll like?" he asked.

"I don't think it'll care," I said.

"Well, I'm not giving it a red one. That's my favourite..."

Tim pulled out a yellow jelly baby and opened the door. Brit rose on its four legs, growling. Little flames of hatred burned in its eyes. Tim took aim and flicked the jelly baby towards its open mouth. The jelly baby hit the bulldog on the nose and bounced off. Brit hurled itself forward and buried its teeth in Tim's bottom.

Tim shrieked and fell backwards into the cell with the dog still clinging on to him. I just hoped he was wearing two pairs of underpants.

Was there anything I could do to help? The dog was in a frenzy, snarling and tugging at Tim, who was lying on his back. I looked around me and saw a bottle of water on the bedside table. I picked it up and in a single continuous movement hit Brit on the head. The bottle smashed. The water splashed. Brit yelped and fell on its side, not dead but dazed. I grabbed hold of Tim and dragged him out of the cell, slamming the door behind us. A second later there was a furious snarling and the scratch of claws against wood. In a way, I was relieved. I can safely say that no animals were harmed in the making of this book.

"Are you all right?" I asked Tim.

"Yes!" He had got to his feet and as far as I could see there was no sign of blood.

"Did he hurt you?" I asked.

"No," he said. "Luckily, I was wearing two pairs of underpants."

"That is lucky," I agreed.

"So what now?"

"We have to find the lift and get back to the cable car."

But that was easier said than done. I've already mentioned that the castle was a labyrinth with twisting corridors and dozens of staircases. The real problem was that they all looked the same. We turned a corner and came to another corner exactly like the one we'd just turned. We passed more suits of armour but were they different suits of armour to the ones we'd seen on our way to the cell? It was impossible to tell. Worse still, we had to keep ducking out of sight whenever we heard anyone coming. We were running out of time. Presumably, Brit was still barking and scratching at the door. It couldn't be too long before someone came to investigate.

We had come to a long passageway with four or five heavy wooden doors and all I knew was that we hadn't been here before. We were about to continue forward when I heard the stamp of feet and two men talking in low voices. We had to get out of sight, and without even thinking I reached for the nearest door and tried to open it. It wouldn't budge but then I noticed a key sticking out of the lock. I turned it, just as two black-suited guards appeared at the far end of the passageway. I grabbed hold of Tim and pulled him inside with me, closing the door without allowing it to slam. I waited breathlessly as the two men walked past.

"Who are you and what are you doing in my room?"

The voice had come from behind us. We wheeled round to see a man in his fifties, dressed in jeans and a loosely knitted jersey. He had long white hair, tied back in a ponytail, and an untidy beard. He was wearing old-fashioned glasses perched on the end of his nose. I'd only ever seen his photograph on Wikipedia, but even without that I'd have known who he was. The clues were all around us. We were in an office with bare bricks, two barred windows and another fireplace. The man was sitting at a table, surrounded by a million pounds' worth of computers and technical equipment: there were screens, metal boxes and wires everywhere, all of them brand new. The last time I had been in a room like this had been in Bath.

The man had to be Alistair Nightingale.

zEbra.

He knew us too. As we stepped forward, his eyes widened. "You're the Diamond brothers!"

"No!" Tim said. "My name's Tim Silver."

"I'm sorry?"

"It's all right, Tim," I cut in. "You don't have to use a fake name. And that's the wrong fake name, by the way. This is the guy we've come to rescue!"

"What? This is Mr Fingernail?"

"He's Alistair Nightingale." I turned back to him. "Is that right? You're zEbra!"

"Yes." The man nodded slowly. "I'm being kept prisoner here. How did you get in?"

"We came through the door," Tim said.

"I mean, how did you get into the castle?"

"It's a long story," I said, then fell silent as I heard footsteps in the corridor – more guards walking past the door. Fortunately, they didn't stop. At the same time, a nasty thought came into my head. "How did you know who we were?" I asked.

"That's easy," Nightingale replied. "I tried to kill you three times."

There was a long silence.

"That's not very nice," Tim said.

"Yes. I'm so sorry."

"Sorry you didn't succeed?" I asked. I was beginning to wish we hadn't come in.

"I'm sorry that I tried. But you have to understand ... Neville Fairfax made me do it. He's a devil. He threatened to kill me if I didn't do what he wanted. He said he'd beat me over the head with a complete volume of his political speeches – or, worse still, he'd make me listen to them. Let me explain..."

I wasn't sure we had the time to listen to all this. Brit would be howling for attention. We had to get moving. But Nightingale had already begun.

"Neville Fairfax snatched me from my home in Bath. You obviously know who I am and what I can do." He held up his hands. "With these ten little soldiers I can break into any computer system in the world – and normally people pay me thousands of pounds for my skills. Not Fairfax. He's not paying me anything – but he says he won't kill me if I give him what he wants."

"And what's that?" Tim asked.

"He wants me to break into the computers that run the UK and then give him full control. If I do what he says, the UK will belong to him. King Neville!" He sighed. "I've been here for a couple of weeks and I've done everything I can to make the whole process as slow as possible. For example, I told them I needed special equipment, which I'd left behind in Bath..."

"The Rubber Ducky!" I said.

"Exactly. I didn't really need it but it wasted time sending his men to go and get it. And that was when I had a bit of luck. The two of you showed up."

"You saw us!" I remembered the CCTV cameras in the house with their blinking red lights. I'd known at the time I was being watched. I just couldn't say who was at the other end.

"That's right. Fairfax was very worried about you."

"He saw us?"

"I showed him the images. Yes."

So how come he didn't recognize us when we went into his office for the interview? I didn't actually ask the question, but the thought sat in my head and refused to leave.

"And then when you showed up at the Archbishop of London's office, he got really nervous. The Archbishop was furious and told Fairfax that the number one priority was to get the two of you out of the way."

"Are you saying the Archbishop of London is working with Fairfax?" I asked.

"The Archbishop and his Chief of Staff, Derek Winslow, are keen supporters of the White Crusaders. They both think Fairfax will make Britain great again. He's promised to close the shops on Sundays and make everyone go to church. If you don't go to church, it's your funeral. And when it's your funeral, you go to church. A win-win situation for Fairfax and his friends."

"Was the Archbishop operating the crane?" Tim asked.

Nightingale gave him a peculiar look. "No!" he said. "Derek Winslow set you up. He sent you over to the building site in Cannon Street and then I took over the crane. It was computer-operated so it was easy to hack into the system and make it drop a steel girder on you."

"It nearly killed us!" I said.

"I had to do it. Fairfax didn't give me any choice. And he didn't stop there. When he heard you'd survived, he made me hack into your phones and your computer. That's how I knew you were meeting Jane Nightingale in that restaurant in Kensington."

"Who is Jane Nightingale?" I asked. "She told us she was your daughter."

"I don't have a daughter."

"Could she be your sister?" Tim said.

"I don't have a sister either. I don't know who she is. Anyway, that was the second time I tried to kill you. I told Tommy and Troy where you were and they went round with their motorbike gang."

"And the third time?" I asked.

"I sent you a fake email inviting you to Battersea Tower. I pretended it came from Jane. Then, once you were there, I hacked into the computer system, which allowed me to control the lights, the doors, the lifts ... just about everything in the building. Once again, I had no choice. Neville Fairfax was standing over me in this very room. I hoped you'd escape ... and I was delighted that you did. It was a really smart move, setting off the sprinkler system."

"Thank you," Tim muttered, as if it had been his idea.

I didn't argue. But I'd just had a nasty thought. Neville Fairfax had ordered Nightingale to kill us. He'd been watching us and listening in to our phone calls. It seemed he'd known about us all along. So why had he welcomed us into the castle and, for that matter, why had he let Tim stay? He must have known that I wasn't a real boot boy. What game was he playing?

Perhaps, if I'd thought about it more, I'd have been able to work it out. But right then, there was only one thought on my mind: we needed to get out of there.

"OK," I said. "You've tried to kill us three times. Is there any chance you could stop yourself trying a fourth time while we rescue you?"

"Is that why you're here?"

"Well, we didn't come for the view," I said.

"Although it is very pretty," Tim added.

"We need to find our way back to the cable car control room," I went on. "Do you have any idea where it is?"

"Sure." Alistair Nightingale turned to the nearest computer and tapped a few keys. I thought it was a strange time to be sending an email but I didn't say anything. He hit ENTER, grabbed his mobile phone and got to his feet. "Follow me," he said. "I can take you there now."

Suddenly, things were looking a little easier. Nightingale was going to take us where we wanted to go. We'd hit the button. Flint and the others would arrive and there wouldn't have to be a massive gunfight. We'd jump into the cable car and we'd be gone before anyone noticed. The helicopter would land and pick us up. With a bit of luck, we'd be back in London in time for tea.

I opened the door and looked out into the corridor. There was nobody in sight.

"This way!" Alistair Nightingale slipped out ahead of me and we set off past more suits of armour and a collection of the weirdest pictures I'd ever seen. The first one showed a fire extinguisher. Next came a one-man submarine. Then there was a bicycle, an army tank, a light bulb, a television set, a toothbrush.

Nightingale must have seen the look on my face. "They're all British inventions," he explained.

Well, that was something I learned from my visit

to Seagull's Rise and in a way, it was actually quite impressive. But it still wouldn't persuade me to join the White Crusaders.

No alarms had gone off yet and I wondered if Brit the bulldog had swallowed the jelly baby after all. We turned a corner, went down a flight of stairs and through an archway. Suddenly, we were there. The industrial lift was ahead of us and it was empty. We stepped in and took it down to the control room.

The doors opened again and there it was. The cable car was parked in its slot right in front of us. I could see the green button in the middle of the console. The control desk had been left unattended. The plump mechanic who had been sitting there when we arrived had gone. He'd left an empty coffee mug and a teaspoon behind.

But even as I ran forward, I was worried. It all seemed too easy. There was a ton of security in the castle. Even the chambermaids carried automatic pistols along with their feather dusters. So why had the most important room of all been abandoned? This was the only way in and out. You'd have thought Neville Fairfax or his head of security would have had guards everywhere.

It was too late now. Tim had reached the green button ahead of me and punched down. He missed the button and hit the teaspoon, which rocketed over his shoulder.

"Wait!" I began. I was sure there was something wrong.

I was too late. He slammed his fist down a second time and now the button connected. The machinery groaned into life, the various cogs and wheels grinding, the metal cylinder turning as it played out the cable connected to the car. The car itself jerked out of its coupling and allowed itself to be dragged towards the exit and the open sky. A moment later, it was on its way, making the journey down to the base of the mountain. We had six minutes. That was how long Flint had said it would take them to arrive.

They were the longest six minutes of my life. Watching the cable car make its way down the mountainside, I was certain that it had decided to travel at half its normal speed and it seemed to take for ever to cross the emerald lake that I had noticed on the way up. Surely somebody in the castle would have noticed it by now? Neville Fairfax's office looked over a courtyard but doubtless he'd hear the cable car moving and would wonder what was going on. And what about Milton Grove? The head of security had said he would be back in an hour but he might already be looking for us. Brit, the battered British bulldog, must have been discovered by now. We were still on our own, but danger could be coming at us from a dozen different directions.

There was a loud *click* as the cylinder stopped turning. The cable car had arrived at the lower station! I could imagine the doors sliding open and Flint, Marcie and Blake clambering in. I remembered the two White Crusaders who had questioned us before we had been allowed up to Seagull's Rise and wondered briefly what had happened to them. I didn't imagine they'd be sending Christmas cards this year, not unless there was a post office at the bottom of the lake.

Twenty seconds limped past. The whole room was silent. And then, with another *click*, the cylinder began to turn again, this time in the opposite direction. Flint and his friends were on their way! I looked out and saw the cable car making its return journey, getting larger and larger as it came into view. After about a minute I could just make out the figure of Flint, sitting, unmoving, on the bench behind the glass. Another minute and the cable car was filling the entranceway and at last it swept into the control room, coming to a halt where it had begun.

The doors slid open. Flint was the first out. In one hand he was carrying the metal suitcase that he had taken from underneath the tarpaulin in the boathouse. The other held a gun. Blake and Marcie were right behind.

Then Flint noticed Alistair Nightingale. "zEbra!" he announced.

"That's me," Nightingale replied.

Flint glanced at me. "Good work, Nick. You found him. That's going to save us a bit of time."

"I found him too!" Tim protested.

We might have argued about it. We might have sat down and discussed who had actually found Nightingale.

But unfortunately, that never happened. Instead, the lift doors opened and Neville Fairfax marched in along with Milton Grove and four armed guards. Suddenly, we found ourselves looking down the muzzles of seven automatic pistols. Fairfax was holding two of them.

"Don't move!" he commanded.

There was nothing we could do. The guards had spread out so that we were covered from all sides. We were outnumbered. Fairfax knew it. He was smiling. He walked forward and snatched Flint's gun.

"You're Flint?" he asked.

Flint scowled. "You don't care what my name is."

"Oh yes I do." Fairfax smiled. "I need to know what to put on the gravestone." He turned to the guards. "Take their weapons off them and bring them up to the courtyard. Is the firing squad ready?"

"They're still in bed," Grove replied.

"OK. They're fired. Get another six guards and tell them to form another firing squad. Tell them to report to the courtyard immediately. They have a job to do."

Breakout

It had been a trap.

I'd begun to work it out when I was in zEbra's room, but I should have seen it from the start. Fairfax and Grove had known all along who we were. That was why the interview had been so short and why Tim had been allowed to stay. Fairfax must have recognized us the moment we walked into his office, but he had pretended otherwise because he wanted us to call Flint, Marcie and Blake up to the castle. He'd made sure that the control room was empty. So, when Tim had hit the green button, he'd unwittingly delivered them all into Fairfax's hands.

While Fairfax and Grove covered them with their own

guns, the four guards removed all the machine guns, pistols, rifles, bayonets, daggers, flick knives, axes, hand grenades, landmines, catapults, slingshots, tasers and coshes that Waverly's agents had brought with them. By the time they'd finished, there were enough weapons on the floor to open a shop. Someone had even brought a harpoon. Strangely enough, nobody had noticed the silver suitcase that Flint had been carrying when he came out of the cable car. He must have set it down the moment he realized he'd walked into an ambush. I noticed it sitting next to the control desk, out of sight, but I didn't say anything.

"Have you got everything?" Fairfax asked.

"Yes, sir!" the guards chorused.

"All right. Let's take them upstairs."

"You don't need me, do you?" Tim asked. "Because if not, I thought I'd head back to London..."

"I'm afraid I do need you, Mr Diamond," Fairfax snarled. "You have an appointment in the courtyard."

Tim stared. "You want me to join the firing squad?"

"No. You're going to be one of the targets."

"That's even worse!"

I was holding out for some last-minute miracle. From the beginning, Flint had known what he was doing. The boathouse had been opened. The new clothes had been waiting for us. The silver case – whatever was inside it – had been concealed. I was certain that he must have something else up his sleeve. I glanced in his direction and saw that his shirt didn't have sleeves. So much for that idea.

"This way, everyone," Fairfax said. "Nightingale, you can watch! And if you haven't cracked the codes by tomorrow morning, we'll shoot you and find somebody else."

"Forget it!" Nightingale shook his head. "I'm not doing your dirty work for you, Fairfax. I'd prefer to die than give you control of the country."

Fairfax scowled. "That's easily arranged," he muttered. He glanced at Grove. "Tell the firing squad to bring an extra bullet."

One of the guards pressed the lift button and the door slid open. For a moment, nobody moved. Out of the corner of my eye I saw Alistair Nightingale slip his hand into his trouser pocket. I wondered if he might have a gun, but when the hand came out it was holding a mobile phone. How was that going to help us? Perhaps he planned to ring his mother and say goodbye.

Fairfax and Grove were the first into the lift. Two of the guards went in with them. The other two stayed, motioning for us to get in with them. Flint hesitated and I didn't blame him. I was in no hurry either.

And then the lift doors began to close.

I saw Grove lean forward and stab the button that would open them again, but it had no effect. The two metal doors continued towards each other and before anyone could do anything, they had met, sealing Fairfax, Grove and two guards inside. That just left the two guards covering us. One of them stepped forward and tapped the button to open the doors. It was a mistake for two reasons. First of all, it didn't work – nothing happened. Also, he had taken his eye off us.

Flint, Blake and Marcie moved at the same moment. Flint grabbed hold of the guard at the lift, seized him by the shoulders and crashed his head into the wall. Marcie lashed out with her foot, driving it into the other guard's stomach and, as he doubled up, Blake took him out with the side of his elbow. The action lasted no more than five seconds but by the end of it, both guards were unconscious. On the other side of the lift doors, I could hear hammering and then a blast of machine-gun fire. It didn't do any good. The doors remained closed.

It was Alistair Nightingale, of course. I'd already worked it out, remembering what had happened at Battersea Tower. Before he left his room, he had pressed some of the keys on his computer and just now he had taken out his phone. He had hacked into the lift control system and closed the doors, and somehow Flint and the others had been expecting it. There was still a lot happening that I didn't completely understand but I wasn't going to stand there and ask questions. The blast of machine-gun fire would have been heard throughout the castle. Other guards would be on their way. We had to get out fast.

"Into the cable car!" Flint shouted and we all set off at a run. I was right behind Marcie and Blake with Nightingale in the lead and the four of us plunged into the cabin, but when I turned round, there was no sign of Tim. For a horrible moment, I thought he'd decided to go and help Fairfax get out of the lift or something equally daft. But then he appeared, sliding in beside me. Flint had picked up one of the machine guns. He swung it over his shoulder, then hit the green button and dashed towards us, leaping into the cable car just as the door slid shut. We were all inside! The cylinder was already turning, the machinery humming. I felt the ground jerk beneath my feet and a few seconds later we were pulled out into the open air. We were on our way down.

It would take us three minutes – one hundred and eighty seconds – before we were safe. I began to count.

Twenty-seven, twenty-eight, twenty-nine...

I could hardly bear to look out of the window at the town far below. With six of us in the cable car, there was less room to move. Nightingale was slumped against the window. He was older than anyone else and he looked worn out. Flint wasn't talking. His eyes were fixed on the castle.

Sixty-one, sixty-two, sixty-three...

We'd made it past the first minute. Fairfax and Grove must still be stuck in the lift and no other guards had yet arrived. It was beginning to look as if we might make it. We were passing over the edge of the emerald lake, which was glistening in the sunlight. I noticed Alistair Nightingale holding his mobile phone, furiously typing. I knew that he had taken control of the computer system in Seagull's Rise. But what was he up to now?

"Is everyone OK?" Flint asked.

Blake and Marcie nodded.

"I think I stubbed my toe getting into the cable car," Tim said.

"You want to go back to get a plaster?" Blake growled.

Tim considered. "No thanks."

Seventy, seventy-one, seventy-two...

Flint looked at his watch. "Five minutes until it goes off," he muttered.

"Five minutes until what goes off?" I asked.

"I left a little something behind. A nice surprise for Fairfax and his friends."

"You mean ... you left it behind on purpose?" Tim asked. He was going rather red and, suddenly, I was worried.

"Yes," Flint said. "I did."

Eighty-four, eighty-five...

Tim glanced down sheepishly. And there, between his feet, was the silver suitcase that Flint had taken from the boathouse and brought to the castle. I remembered that Tim hadn't run straight into the cable car. That must have been when he picked it up.

"What have you done?" Flint whispered in horror.

"I thought you'd forgotten it," Tim whimpered.

"I picked it up for you. I thought you'd be pleased."

"You idiot! Do you have any idea what you've done?" Flint grabbed the silver case, picked it up and opened it. For the first time I saw what it contained. There were about a dozen sticks of dynamite all taped together, a tangle of different coloured wires, some complicated-looking circuit boards and an alarm clock that was ticking to twelve o'clock. "This is a bomb," he explained. "I was using it to blow up the castle."

Tim was on the edge of tears. "Why didn't you tell me?" he asked. He glanced at his watch. "Do we have time to take it back?"

Ninety-seven, ninety-eight, ninety-nine...

And then the cable car stopped. It was actually quite shocking, the sudden lack of movement. The six of us hung in the air, swaying back and forth.

"What now?" Blake asked.

"They must have got out of the lift," Flint muttered. "They've stopped the cable car from up in the control room."

The bomb was primed. The alarm clock was ticking. Fairfax and his men had us exactly where they wanted us: we were hanging there like a puppet on a chain. And any minute now the cable car with all six of us in it was going to be blown to pieces.

This definitely wasn't my day.

Mr Whippy

"So, what do we do now?" I asked.

To be honest, there wasn't very much we could do. Everything was silent as we hung there, fifty metres above the ground. The castle was above us. The town, slightly nearer, was below. But we weren't going anywhere. A couple of seagulls wheeled past as if they wanted to know what was going on, then lost interest and flew away.

The bomb in the suitcase was still ticking.

"I don't suppose you can turn that thing off?" I asked.

Flint shook his head. "Once it's activated, there's nothing I can do," he said.

"Suppose you change the time...?"

"That won't work. If I even touch the clock, it will blow up."

"So how much time do we have?"

Flint glanced at the clock face. It showed four minutes to twelve. "Four minutes," he said.

"Oh look!" Tim said. He had his face pressed against the window. "You can see Scotland from here."

That was great. We had four minutes to live and Tim was enjoying the view. He seemed to have forgotten that he was the one who had brought the bomb into the cable car. If Flint's plan had worked, it would have been left behind in the control centre, which would have blown up after we'd arrived back at ground level. He could see Scotland! In four minutes' time, half of him would probably be *in* Scotland.

Suddenly, there was a jerk and the cable car began to move again.

"Thank goodness for that!" Tim exclaimed.

"I don't think so..." I said.

We weren't going down. We were going back up.

What had happened? Neville Fairfax had obviously taken control of the situation and had made sure we weren't going to get away. His firing squad was waiting for us ... not that there would be very much left to aim at if the bomb went off before we arrived. Whatever came next, it looked as if we were finished. Slowly, painfully, we were being drawn back into Seagull's Rise.

But Flint had a plan. He had lifted the machine gun off his shoulder and was cradling it, pointing the muzzle at the cable car door. Amazingly, he'd found the time to light a cigar. "Stand back!" he called out.

We all got out of the way and he pressed the trigger, sending a stream of bullets into the glass. The noise in the confined space was deafening and a dense, bitter smell filled the interior. But Flint had done what he set out to do. The wind rushed in. A whole side of the cable car had been demolished. Take two steps forward and we'd fall to the ground far below ...

... which was exactly the idea! With a horrible

feeling in my stomach, I saw that we were about half-way across the emerald lake that I had noticed on the way up. How deep was it? If the answer wasn't "very", we were in trouble. The lake was a long, long way down and the water did not look warm.

"All right!" Flint shouted. "Jump in the lake!"

"I don't see why you have to be so rude!" Tim muttered.

Flint grabbed him. "Now!" He gave Tim a push and with a last, desperate squeal, Tim disappeared from sight.

Marcie and Blake went next with Nightingale between them. Flint looked at me as I edged my way over the broken glass and towards the shattered door. "Break a leg," he said.

Was he joking?

I jumped.

If you can imagine the highest diving board you've ever seen – the sort of diving board that you see at the Olympic Games – and then add ten more diving boards of the same height on top of it, that was where

I'd started and that was how far I had to fall. Was the water actually underneath me? I didn't dare look down. In fact, I'm not sure I'd have been able to anyway. It was as if I'd been shot, feet first, out of a cannon. My whole body was rocketing through the cold mountain air and the only direction I was going was down. Someone was yelling and it took me a few seconds to realize it was me. Vaguely, I was aware of the ground rushing up to meet me. What was it going to be? Water or earth? Splash or smash? In about half a second I would find out.

I hit the water. At that very last moment, I got the sense that I had jumped onto a giant green mirror and I could see my own reflection with a grin, which might have been enjoyment but was more probably terror. Somewhere behind, over my shoulder, I glimpsed Flint falling towards the same spot. He must have jumped immediately after me. Then I was through, out of this world and into a dark, freezing swirl of water and ice. At least I'd remembered to hold my breath. I kept going down but slower and slower as the lake seized hold of me. Then I was rising, with bubbles exploding from my mouth and my lungs reminding me that they preferred having air. I broke through the surface and gasped, brilliant drops of water cascading out of my hair. My body felt as if it had been pulverized. But I was alive.

I managed to recover a little and looked around. The first thing I saw was Tim, treading water about five metres away. He hadn't noticed that there was a large clump of seaweed on his head. Marcie and Blake were already swimming for the shore, guiding Alistair between them. Behind me, Flint broke through the surface and to my astonishment I saw that there was a cigar still clenched between his teeth.

"Move it!" he shouted.

He was looking up. I followed his eyes and saw Seagull's Rise high above and the cable car slowly gliding towards it – and that was when it hit me. Neville Fairfax had ordered the cable car to be brought back up, but he hadn't realized that it was carrying a suitcase with a dozen sticks of dynamite. Now it was just a question of time. Right then, I forgot that I had just survived a leap from a terrifying height and that I was treading water in a freezing lake. All I could do was watch. The little cabin, with no passengers and one side shattered by machine-gun fire, had almost reached the end of the line. I saw it sweep into the control room.

And then it exploded. A brilliant fireball shot out, followed by an enormous bang a couple of seconds later. I didn't think Fairfax or Grove would have much to say after that. But it wasn't over yet. The blast must have done something to the foundations of Seagull's Rise. As the smoke cleared, the entire structure seemed to slide towards the edge of the mountain and then, right in front of my eyes, it disintegrated, falling into space. No wonder Flint had shouted at me to get moving. It looked as if the whole thing was going to fall on top of me. Fortunately, there was just enough space between the edge of the mountain and the shoreline. A hundred thousand bricks, tons of glass, furniture and marble fireplaces, fifty suits of armour, a collection of weird pictures and a million pounds' worth of computer equipment came crashing down in a huge heap. A few bits and pieces splashed into the water. Smoke and dust rose into the air.

And do you know what? There was a part of me that was a little sad. At the very least, I felt sorry for Brit, the blown-up British bulldog.

I began to swim, following Flint to the shore. I was the last out of the lake and stood there, shivering, wondering what was going to happen next. We had escaped from the castle but we were still on Hare Island and the roar of distant motorbikes, somewhere in the town, told me that we still needed to get to safety. There were the police and the White Crusaders to deal with. Maybe Fairfax had called them while we were still in the cable car. In any event, they were already on their way.

"Over here!" Flint shouted and for the first time I noticed a dilapidated wooden barn just beside the lake. Marcie was already there, pulling open the doors, and I realized that – like the boathouse beside the beach – they had known it was there all along and it was part of their plan. I hurried towards it, catching up with Tim.

"Oh look!" he said. "We can have an ice cream!"

For once, he hadn't gone completely mad. There was a van parked inside the barn, painted pink and white with a sign reading "MR WHIPPY" mounted on the roof. One side was given over to a large serving window. It was an ice-cream van. Had it really been parked here for us?

Even Flint was surprised. "What the hell...?" he demanded.

"It was all we could get," Blake said.

I could hear the motorbikes getting closer. There was no time to argue.

"Get in!" Flint snarled.

We all piled into the ice-cream van. Marcie was driving. Flint sat next to her – still cradling the machine gun. He must have carried it with him when he jumped out of the cable car. Alistair Nightingale, Blake, Tim and I were standing in the back, surrounded by freezers and chill cabinets. Marcie pushed the gear into reverse and backed out of the barn.

"Take it slowly," Flint growled. "And everyone keep quiet. We don't want to draw attention to ourselves."

The ice-cream van bumped over a pothole. Tim wasn't holding on to anything and lost his balance.

Before I could stop him, he fell onto the dashboard and his elbow jammed into a button. At once, the ice-cream van's chimes started up, ringing out at full volume.

"Turn that off!" Marcie snapped.

Flint reached for the control. "He's broken it!" he exclaimed.

With the chimes still sounding, the little van bumped round the side of the lake and down a grass slope to the main road. The four of us in the back were thrown from side to side, but then we felt concrete under the tyres and the ride became smoother. But not safer. Looking out of the back window, I could see nine or ten White Crusaders speeding towards us. I recognized two of them. Tommy and Troy had been at Alistair Nightingale's house in Bath and had followed us to Grannies in Kensington. They had been outside the police station in Battersea when Assistant Chief Commissioner Davina Dawson had forced us to leave. It was somehow no surprise that they had turned up now.

And they had almost caught up with us! They were so close that I could see the hairs in their nostrils ... not a pleasant sight at any time. I watched as they reached behind them, drawing guns from out of their waistbands. The other motorbikers had spread out like an arrow, stretching across the road.

Flint leaned out of the window and fired a burst of bullets with the machine gun. He was aiming at the tyres and, sure enough, a few of the Crusaders' bikes slewed to one side, throwing the riders into the long grass. But then the gun fell silent. "I'm out of ammo," Flint snarled. He threw the gun out of the window. It hit one of the bikers on the head and knocked him off his bike. At least that brought the count down to six.

And still the chimes were playing, advertising the ice cream that we weren't going to sell. It had all melted, anyway. Whoever had stolen the Mr Whippy van had left the freezers and chill cabinets full of vanilla and

chocolate ice cream, Twisters, choc ices and Cornettos. As Marcie hit the accelerator and we picked up speed, the music changed. It was playing the theme from *Star Wars* arranged for tinkling bells, and although Flint was now stamping on the off button with the heel of his boot, he couldn't stop it.

After the attack with the machine gun, we'd pulled ahead, putting a bit of distance between the van and the remaining motorbikes. The road was running right next to the sea now, about ten metres above it. There was no fence, just a sandy cliff that cut down to the water's edge. Marcie was driving as fast as she could, but the ice-cream van's engine was no match for the Harley-Davidsons behind us. It was obvious that, in seconds, the White Crusaders would catch up with us again. They all had their guns out. But we had no more weapons.

"What are we going to do?" I cried.

"Can I have a Cornetto?" Tim asked.

"No!"

"Just one!"

"No, Tim!" But for once my big brother had given

me an idea. I reached into the chill cabinet and pulled out a plastic tub of melted ice cream. "Open the back door!" I shouted.

Blake understood what I wanted to do. He reached out and opened the doors so that I could see the road rushing past behind us. I threw out the plastic tub, then took two more and Blake did the same. Alistair Nightingale joined in and even Tim got the idea so that in the next few seconds a dozen ice-cream tubs had hit the road, spreading their contents across the tarmac. Tommy and Troy were the first to reach the brightly coloured puddles. I saw their faces change as their bikes skidded and they lost control. First they crashed into each other. Then they bounced apart and shot off the road. Tommy hit a tree. Troy disappeared over the side of the cliff and plunged into the sea.

We had no more ice cream. There were still four motorbikers coming after us and then Tim cried out. I turned round and saw that it had all been hopeless after all.

The road ended.

We had travelled from one end of Hare Island to the other. Ahead of us there was a low red-and-white barrier with a tangle of barbed wire and, beyond that, a narrow beach with the sea lapping at the sand. We had nowhere else to go. I felt the ice-cream van slow down and stop. Finally, the chimes fell silent. Behind us, the remaining White Crusaders spread out. They had survived the ice cream. They had guessed we were unarmed. As we came to a halt, they did the same,

climbing off their bikes and moving towards us. All of them were armed, two of them with machine guns. This time, they weren't taking any chances.

A solitary seagull flew overhead as if it had come to witness the climax. I saw it out of the corner of my eye as the first bikers raised their guns. The seagull hovered, then suddenly darted away. Something had frightened it. A second later, the road erupted in a series of miniature explosions, dust and broken tarmac leaping up.

At the same time, I heard the sound of rotors pounding at the sky and out of nowhere a helicopter appeared, slanting towards us. A figure in a camouflage jacket was sitting with his legs dangling, firing his own machine gun at the White Crusaders. The four of them scrabbled for their bikes. They managed to get them started as the helicopter hovered over them, filling the entire sky. The bikers twisted their machines around and roared off the way they had come. The helicopter lowered itself slowly, delicately and landed on the beach.

It wasn't meant to arrive until four o'clock, which was still hours away. How had the pilot known to come early? I saw Alistair Nightingale smiling and remembered that he had sent a text message when we were in the cable car.

"It was you!" I shouted. "You called the helicopter!"

He didn't even try to deny it. "Things happened a little faster than I'd expected."

So Alistair Nightingale had *known* he was going to be rescued. He had been expecting us all along. He had even known who Tim and I were when we entered his room. He must have known about Flint, Marcie and Blake too. He had been the one who had trapped Neville Fairfax and the others in the lift. He wasn't some kind of innocent victim ... he was part of the team.

But this wasn't the time to ask questions. We all piled out of the ice-cream van and headed down to the beach. I allowed myself to be bundled into the helicopter with Tim and waited for the rotors to pick up speed. Suddenly, we were rising into the air, leaving Hare Island far behind.

The Double Agent

It ended two days later in London, back in Mr Waverly's office.

We had said goodbye to Flint, Marcie and Blake at the London helicopter pad where we'd landed, and I can't say I was too sorry to see them go. They'd been lying to us all along. They'd used Tim and me to help get them into Seagull's Rise but we'd never been part of the team. I had the feeling that the two of us had been counters in a board game but nobody had bothered to explain the rules. We were just lucky that the dice had rolled the right way. Somehow we'd made it to the last square.

Mr Waverly was in his usual place, behind his desk. Fiona Duncan-Jones, the woman who was about to take over as head of MI6, was sitting to one side. This time she was dressed in a dark suit with a leather handbag on her lap. One leg was crossed over the other with a black leather shoe dangling beside her ankle.

Alistair Nightingale was also in the room but he looked completely different. For a start, he'd had a haircut. The ponytail was gone, as was the beard. He no longer needed glasses and instead of jeans and a sweater, he was wearing a suit. There were two empty seats for Tim and me. As we sat down, Waverly smiled. That was unusual. It was almost as if he was pleased to see us.

"Thank you for coming," he began. He'd telephoned us that morning and asked us to come in. Of course, if we'd refused, we'd have been knocked out or held at gunpoint and brought here anyway, but he was too polite to mention it.

"It's a pleasure," I said, a little sourly.

"No, it isn't!" Tim scowled. We were both having

nightmares about the jump from the cable car; the night before, he'd sleepwalked into the kitchen and thrown himself out of the window. It was just lucky we were on the ground floor.

"I understand it was quite a nasty experience for you," Waverly agreed. "Which is why I thought you might like to know the truth about what actually happened at Seagull's Rise."

"Yeah," I said. I pointed at Nightingale. "Why don't we start with him? I'm guessing that he works for you."

"That's right," Waverly said.

"And he isn't who he says he is."

"What?" Tim stared. "Are you saying he isn't Alistair Fingernail?"

"He may be called Alistair Nightingale," I replied. "But he isn't zEbra."

"Is that true?" Fiona Duncan-Jones sounded shocked. I was surprised by that. She was Waverly's number two. She must have known what he had been planning.

"Our young friend is absolutely correct," Waverly

said. "I'm afraid I have a lot to explain, and to understand it, we have to go back to the beginning."

"You mean, when the world was created?" Tim asked.

"Not quite as far back as that, no. I mean the moment when Neville Fairfax decided he wanted to take over the UK." Waverly took out a pipe but he didn't light it. I guessed he just liked the feel of it in his hands. "It should be obvious to you that Fairfax believed in the very worst sort of politics. It's one thing to want to make Britain great, but that doesn't mean you have to hate people who aren't British. And the idea of taking over the government, starting a war ... well, it soon became clear that he was extremely dangerous.

"The trouble is, there were a great many people who supported him and who did everything they could to help him. These were powerful people in the Church, in the police, in government, in the press ... even here, in MI6."

"We haven't been able to prove that," Fiona Duncan-Jones reminded him.

"That's true." Waverly nodded. "It's something that's been worrying us a great deal – the idea that Fairfax had a double agent working here, telling him our secrets and stopping us from getting to the truth. So we came up with a plan!"

"And what was that?" Tim asked.

"I'm about to tell you."

"Go ahead," I said, quietly stamping on Tim's foot.

"We heard that Fairfax was looking for a major computer hacker who goes by the name of zEbra. We'd been interested in zEbra ourselves. In fact, there wasn't an intelligence agency in the world that wasn't searching for him. The man was a genius but there was no saying what he might do next. We couldn't find him and we were fairly sure that Fairfax wouldn't be able to find him either. And that was what gave us our idea."

For the first time, Waverly turned to Alistair Nightingale. "This gentleman is a senior analyst and programmer at GCHQ, Cheltenham. You may remember that I told you that Fairfax actually hoped to break into the computers at Cheltenham. We told

Mr Nightingale about the danger and he very kindly offered to help us fight back."

"Why didn't you tell me any of this?" Fiona Duncan-Jones demanded. She wasn't looking happy at all.

"It was classified," Waverly replied. "You would have been briefed when you took over, of course." He turned back to us. "This was the plan. First of all, Mr Nightingale pretended to be zEbra. We put him into a house in Bath. We filled it with computer equipment. We arranged for Fairfax to find out where he was living and then we waited for the kidnap to happen."

Nightingale picked up the story. "Then Fairfax sent a gang of his White Crusaders," he began. "They snatched me and took me to Hare Island. Once I got there, he threatened to kill me unless I hacked into the government computers. But actually, what he never guessed was that I was there to hack into *his* computers. Do you see? It was the only way we could find out who was working for him."

"I don't get it," Tim said.

"Don't worry, Tim," I said. "I'll explain it all to you

again later." I turned to Waverly. "Fairfax had all the names you wanted in his computer system. But the computers were all inside a heavily guarded castle on an island. So, the only way for you to get your guy inside was to arrange for him to be kidnapped."

"That's exactly right," Waverly said. He smiled again. "Maybe you should think of becoming a spy when you leave school."

"That's a ridiculous idea," I said.

"Why?"

"You haven't seen my reports!"

"Actually, I have."

That was a scary thought. "Maybe I should become a double agent," I said. "Then I'd get paid twice."

Waverly twisted the pipe in his hands. "A double agent was exactly what we were looking for," he said. "It took Mr Nightingale a few weeks to hack into Fairfax's computer. He also had to deal with the two of you, as I'm sure he's explained."

"Deal with us? You mean – try to kill us!"

At least Waverly was decent enough to look

embarrassed. "Yes. I'm sorry about that. But what matters is that the two of you are safe. And in the end we got the information we needed. We now know that the Archbishop of London and his Chief of Staff, Derek Winslow, are both working for Fairfax. So is Assistant Chief Commissioner Davina Dawson. We have a list of twenty other prominent people who are all White Crusaders. Nine of them are government ministers!"

"And what about the double agent inside MI6?" I asked.

"Yes, I'd like to know that," Fiona Duncan-Jones said. She looked as if she was about to be sick.

"I have the name right here," Alistair Nightingale said. He took out a piece of paper and placed it on the desk.

Fiona Duncan-Jones looked down. The name was hers.

"I'm afraid it's all over, Fiona," Waverly said. He pointed the stem of the pipe at her. "We know you're a traitor. You told Fairfax about the house in Bath and you helped him kidnap zEbra. Except it wasn't zEbra. I'm afraid we tricked you all along."

Fiona had got to her feet. I hadn't seen her open her handbag, but suddenly, there was a small black pistol in her hand. She was pointing it at Waverly. "I'm walking out of here," she snarled. "If you try and stop me, I'll put a bullet in your head."

"You're not going anywhere," Waverly replied. The pipe jerked in his hands and Fiona reeled back, shocked. I saw that there was a tiny dart stuck in

her neck. A coil of smoke rose from the stem of Waverly's pipe. Fiona collapsed.

The pipe was a gadget! It had fired a knock-out dart. And I thought that sort of thing only existed in James Bond movies.

"Well, that about wraps it all up," Waverly said. "Ms Duncan-Jones will be spending the rest of her life behind bars."

"She's going to become a cocktail waitress?" Tim asked.

"No. She's going to jail." The spymaster turned to me. "Let me know if you decide to become a spy, Nicholas," he said. "You'll need to get eight A-stars in your GCSEs. Don't worry about revising. We'd actually prefer you to steal the exams and take photographs of the questions. It'll be good training for the future."

"I'll think about it," I said.

But I wouldn't. I'd had enough of agents and double agents, explosions and gunfire. I just wanted to go home.

zEbra

It ended the way it had begun – with a knock at the door.

I wasn't in a great mood. We'd done all that work for Mr Waverly – getting his people into Seagull's Rise and helping rescue Alistair Nightingale – and we'd been paid exactly nothing. There were still five weeks of the summer holidays but we weren't going anywhere. Tim had looked at his bank account online. There was just £17.25 left from the money we'd been paid by "Jane Nightingale" – not enough to take us to France or even Cornwall. If we wanted a holiday, we might just make it to Euston station, which was the next stop on the tube line, but when we got there, we wouldn't be able to afford a train. We'd managed to fill up the fridge so we weren't going to starve, but we had nothing to look forward to apart from lunch.

In fact, we were just finishing breakfast when we heard the knocking, and this time we didn't even try to tidy up the office. The door opened and somehow I wasn't surprised when Jane Nightingale walked back in. She was exactly how I remembered her: those amazing blue eyes, the perfect hair, the smile that could either melt your heart or break it. I wondered what she was doing here. She couldn't have come to thank us for helping find her father because, as we both knew by now, Alistair Nightingale wasn't her dad. Maybe she was going to invite Tim out for dinner. More likely, she wanted her money back.

"Hello," she said. "Can I come in?"

"You already are in," I growled. Suddenly, I was angry. It was thanks to her that we'd just had the worst few days of our life, hunted down by Neville Fairfax and the White Crusaders and almost killed in lots of different ways. The last time we'd seen her, when we'd been trapped at Grannies restaurant, she'd run off and abandoned us. She'd lied to us from the start too.

But here she was, smiling as if nothing had happened. She took a step forward and sat down. Meanwhile, Tim had taken his place behind the desk.

I decided to get straight to the point. "I know who you are," I said.

"Of course you do," Tim said. "I'm your brother."

"Yes, Tim. But I'm not talking to you. I'm talking to her."

"Jane Nightingale."

It was the first time he'd ever got her name right. It was just a shame it was the wrong name.

"That's what she called herself," I said. "But it's not who she is." I turned to her. "You're zEbra, aren't you?"

She didn't look surprised. "So you've worked it out!"

"Wait a minute! Wait a minute!" Tim cut in. He still hadn't completely understood Mr Waverly's explanation about what had happened, even though I'd gone over it half a dozen times. And here was yet another twist that he had to take on board. "That's not possible!"

"The clues were there the very first time we met her," I insisted. "She was wearing a white earring and a black earring ... like a zebra!"

Tim looked at me with a frown on his face. "Zebras don't wear earrings," he said.

"But they're black and white, Tim. When we met at the restaurant, she was wearing a black jacket and a white cap. The same thing. She also has a tattoo on her wrist. I thought it was a lightning strike but I was wrong. It's a letter 'Z'. As in 'Z' for zEbra."

"But what did she want? Why did she come to us?"

I turned to zEbra.

"OK. I'll tell you the truth," she said.

"Why don't you start with your real name?" I suggested.

"I can't tell you that. You have to understand, I've made a lot of enemies. All over the world, there are people spying on each other and they use computer hackers like me to break into each other's security systems. But the trouble is, I know too many secrets. Right now, I've got the intelligence agencies of seventeen different countries searching for me. They're scared of me because of what I can do. More than that, they're scared about what I already know.

"I live my entire life in hiding ... off-grid. I'm not going to tell you my name. I'm not going to tell you where I live. After today, you're never going to see me again."

"Well, that's one bit of good news," I muttered.

"I can understand why you're angry with me, Nick. Let me explain what happened." She drew a breath. "It all started when I heard that there was a computer hacker who called himself zEbra, living in Bath. Of course, that was impossible. It had to be someone pretending to be me. I wondered what he was doing so I went down to see him ... only to discover that he had been kidnapped. That was why I came to you. I had to know what was going on. Who was this man, Alistair Nightingale? Why had he stolen my name and who had snatched him? I was also worried. Once whoever it was discovered that he wasn't the real zEbra, they might come after me.

"That was why I turned to you. I needed a private eye who could get some answers for me and I chose the best!"

"That's another lie!" I said. "If you're as clever as you say you are, you must have known that Tim was the worst private detective in England."

"That's not necessarily true..." Tim muttered.

She nodded. "All right. I admit it. I knew Tim was completely useless. I'd read all about your other cases. I knew you wouldn't question who I was and, at the same time, I needed you to draw the enemy's fire."

"In other words, you needed a target," I said, gloomily. It wasn't the first time it had happened. It was as if Tim had gone through his whole life with a bullseye painted on his back.

She nodded. "That's right. Whoever had kidnapped the fake zEbra would come chasing after you and that would make it easier for me to find out who they were." She smiled. "I've been watching you from the very start. I hacked into your computer and your phones. I could have hacked into your microwave oven if I'd wanted to."

Tim's face had fallen when he heard all this and I realized he still fancied zEbra, despite everything that had happened. Just for once I felt the need to come to his defence. "You may say he's completely useless," I said, "but he always solves the cases in the end."

"With your help!" zEbra reminded me.

"He only helps a little bit," Tim said.

"Well, I won't argue with you." zEbra stood up. "I just wanted to thank you for what you've done. You might like to know that I hacked into your bank account before I came here."

"Why?" I couldn't believe she'd told us that. "What was the point?"

"Open the account and you'll see the point. Goodbye." She smiled one last time. "If you ever need me, just call my name. I'll be listening."

And with that, she walked out of the room.

As soon as she had gone, I swung my laptop round and went straight to Tim's bank account. We both stared at the screen.

"That's..." Tim began.

"Yes, Tim."

"That's..." He couldn't finish the sentence. He was pointing at the screen. His face had gone white.

You'll see the point. That was what zEbra had said. And she'd meant it. Instead of £17.25, she'd moved the decimal point so that Tim now had £172,500,000 in his account. One hundred and seventy-two million, five hundred thousand!

Twenty minutes later, Tim was still stretched out on the floor where he'd fainted. Meanwhile, I was sitting at his desk, deep in thought. Had zEbra stolen the money or had she created it? Would the bank notice? Would we be allowed to keep it?

It had been a strange adventure. Nobody had been what they seemed. Alistair Nightingale hadn't been zEbra. Jane Nightingale hadn't been his daughter. Fiona Duncan-Jones had been a double agent. Mr Waverly hadn't told us the truth about his plans, and Flint, Marcie and Blake had gone along with the lie. None of it had been true.

And now we were multimillionaires. Except we probably weren't. I couldn't wait to find out.

COLLECT ALL OF THE HILARIOUS
DIAMOND BROTHERS INVESTIGATIONS

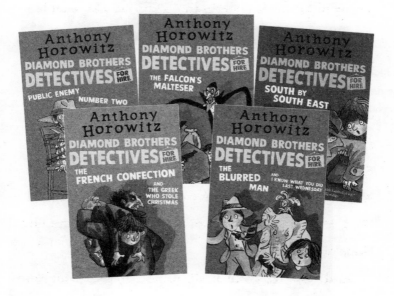

Tim Diamond is the world's worst private detective,
and unfortunately for his quick-thinking brother, Nick,
the cases keep coming in. What connects them?
Murder! And if the Diamond brothers don't play
their cards right, they could be next!

"Horowitz is the perfect writer.
His dialogue crackles with hardboiled wit."
Frank Cottrell Boyce, *Guardian*

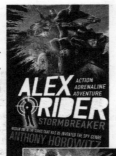
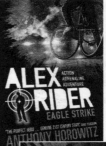

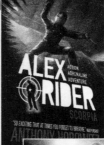

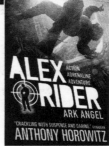

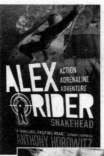
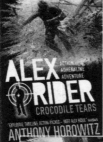
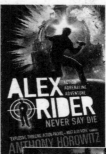
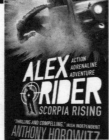

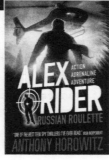
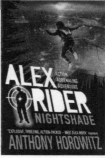

Photograph © Jon Cartwright

Anthony Horowitz is one of the most prolific writers working in the UK, and is unique for working in so many areas – juggling books, TV series, films, plays and journalism. Anthony has written over 50 books, including the bestselling Alex Rider teen spy series, which is estimated to have sold 21 million copies worldwide and has been filmed for Amazon TV.

Anthony is also an acclaimed writer for adults and was commissioned to write two new Sherlock Holmes novels: *The House of Silk* and *Moriarty*. He has written two James Bond novels, *Trigger Mortis* and *Forever and a Day*, and he has a third – *With a Mind to Kill* – coming out in 2022.

Anthony's TV work includes the award-winning *Foyle's War*, *Midsomer Murders*, *Collision* and *Injustice*. He adapted his own novel, *Magpie Murders*, with Lesley Manville in the lead role. Anthony is working on a new murder mystery television series: *Nine Bodies in a Mexican Morgue*.

Anthony is proud to be a patron of the charity Suffolk Home-Start. He has been awarded a CBE for services to literature.

You can find out more about Anthony and his work at:
www.alexrider.com
@AnthonyHorowitz